Javier stopped Carla by pressing his lips against hers, hot and hard, and then pulled away before temptation got out of hand. 'Take the night, think about it, and give me your answer in the morning. I know you'll choose wisely.'

'You're so certain you know what I'll decide?'

He shrugged. 'Besides the pleasure you'll receive in my bed, there's the added benefit that once your father knows you're mine—truly mine—he'll think twice about threatening you again.'

'So those are my choices? Choose you or choose him?'

'The writing's been on the wall for a while, Principessa. This way you know you're backing the right horse.'

He flung the door open and grabbed her hand. In the bright light of the foyer he caught a clearer glimpse of her outfit and cursed himself for giving her the night to agree to his demands. The ache in his groin alone threatened to fracture his mind.

Although his every instinct screamed at him to go after her, when she'd muttered goodnight and made a beeline for her bedroom Javier stayed put.

Morning would come soon enough.

Carla Nardozzi would be his.

Maya Blake's hopes of becoming a writer were born when she picked up her first romance at thirteen. Little did she know her dream would come true! Does she still pinch herself every now and then to make sure it's not a dream? Yes, she does! Feel free to pinch her, too, via Twitter, Facebook or Goodreads! Happy reading!

Don't miss *A Diamond Deal with the Greek* featuring Draco and Rebel from *Signed Over to Santino* available now!

Books by Maya Blake

Mills & Boon Modern Romance

Married for the Prince's Convenience
Innocent in His Diamonds
His Ultimate Prize
Marriage Made of Secrets
The Sinful Art of Revenge
The Price of Success

Secret Heirs of Billionaires

Brunetti's Secret Son

The Untameable Greeks

What the Greek's Money Can't Buy
What the Greek Can't Resist
What the Greek Wants Most

The 21st Century Gentleman's Club

The Ultimate Playboy

Visit the Author Profile page
at millsandboon.co.uk for more titles.

SIGNED OVER TO SANTINO

BY
MAYA BLAKE

First Published in Great Britain 2016
By Mills & Boon, an imprint of HarperCollins*Publishers*
1 London Bridge Street, London, SE1 9GF

© 2016 Maya Blake

ISBN: 978-0-263-06464-3

Our policy is to use papers that are natural, renewable and recyclable products and made from wood grown in sustainable forests. The logging and manufacturing processes conform to the legal environmental regulations of the country of origin.

Printed and bound in Great Britain
by CPI Antony Rowe, Chippenham, Wiltshire

SIGNED OVER
TO SANTINO

PROLOGUE

CARLA NARDOZZI TOOK the chauffeur's proffered hand, stepped out of the luxury SUV and was immediately bombarded with the sights and sounds of New York City. The journey from her Upper East Side hotel to Midtown had been as tense and chilly as the air conditioning blasting from the vents.

To her right, her father, Olivio Nardozzi, stood stiff and seething.

Carla would've summoned a genuine smile for the driver had she been able to function in anything other than a complete state of ongoing shock.

The past seven days had unfolded in a series of bombshells she could scarcely wrap her head around. Bombshells she'd struggled to navigate without going under until she'd eventually, exhausted, settled in a place of icy numbness. But the biggest trial of all lay ahead of her. Or more accurately, it lay above her, sixty-six floors up in the office of the man she'd hoped never to set eyes on again.

As if pulled by powerful magnets, her gaze slid up the glass façade of the building housing the esteemed J Santino Inc.

An opportunity beyond your wildest dreams.

A once-in-a-lifetime endorsement deal.

A collaboration even a figure skater with your prominence would be insane to turn down.

For the better part of a year, those words had been impressed upon her by her father and her advisors. Lately, they'd been uttered in the solemn, no-nonsense tones of her agent and friend, Draco Angelis, who'd been at a loss as to why she was resisting the life-changing deal.

She'd listened and nodded in all the right places but had

known she would never accept the deal. Never have anything to do with the man heading the globally successful luxury goods company.

She'd kept her secret for three years and Carla had had no intention of facing it, or the man it involved, ever.

Until her reality had drastically altered.

A shiver that had nothing to do with the blustery March spring day rattled her bones.

In a few minutes, after long years of strictly regimented avoidance, she would be face to face with Javier Santino.

The man who'd taken her virginity. The man who'd granted her the most sensual, intensely unforgettable night of her life. The man who'd then absorbed her shocked, poorly delivered words the morning after with granite-faced hatred, then proceeded to banish her from his life with the cold incisiveness of a scalpel-wielding surgeon.

Years later, Carla still couldn't recall those harrowing hours without the naked blade of fear striking her heart.

It was the reason she'd avoided Javier Santino at all costs. It was the reason this was the last place she would've willingly placed herself.

'Come on, the deal isn't going to finalise itself with you standing out here staring at the building.'

The numbness that had wrapped itself tightly around her eased for a cracked moment, replaced with myriad volatile emotions as she stared at her father. Disappointment. Sadness. Anger. A deep and painful burgeoning acceptance that Olivio Nardozzi had a vastly differing definition of parental love than most normal fathers had for their children.

Bitterness surged high. 'We wouldn't be here if you hadn't gambled away—'

'Don't start this again, Carla.' He stepped closer on the busy sidewalk so they wouldn't be overheard by the trio of lawyers who'd accompanied them and now stood on the sidewalk, ready to escort her into Javier's presence. 'We have aired this out many times already. I don't particularly want to air it once again, especially in public. You have an image to maintain. A faultless image we have *both* worked hard for. In less than an hour's time, our financial worries will be on their way to being a thing of the past. We have to look forward.'

Look forward.

How could she when her immediate future entailed placing herself in the heart of the lion's den? A lion whose deathly silence had been even more unnerving than the roar she'd expected at any point during these past three years?

Sucking in a shaky breath, she placed one foot in front of the other, walked through the revolving doors and stood in the lift as they were whisked upward.

The office décor of J Santino Inc. was the last thing Carla expected. Sure, the place pulsed with the core efficiency needed to run a billion-dollar enterprise. But while Carla had expected glass and chrome and futuristic art pieces, she exited the lift and stepped into a vibrant foyer with colourful walls, exotic flowers and employees relaxing on lounge chairs and giant futons. Exquisite Latin American art dotted the vast space, and she was unwillingly reminded of Javier's passionate Spanish side.

Closing her mind to it, she followed a statuesque receptionist down a burgundy-carpeted hallway to a set of wide double doors, which swung open with an electric whine.

'Mr Santino will be with you in a moment.'

Carla's heart climbed into her throat as she entered a vast conference room.

Absently, she heard murmurs as her team took their seats, but she couldn't think past the coming meeting, her insides twisting hard as she drifted past sumptuous chairs and a polished cherry-oak table towards wide windows with impressive views of Manhattan.

Would those gold-brown eyes that had snapped cold fire at her the last time they'd seen her still blaze with hatred? Over the last year, since she'd first been approached with the endorsement offer, she'd wondered why Javier Santino would want her anywhere near his company. Sure, her world-number-one-figure-skater status placed her in a certain *would-kill-for* echelon, but there were a few dozen other sports figures in a similar position. Despite her management's insistence that she was being pursued because she was the right person for the job, she'd wondered whether it'd been a carefully set trap.

But not once had Javier attempted personal contact, choosing to communicate through his lawyers and executives. Folding her arms, Carla swallowed and allowed a little hope to grow. Maybe Javier had moved past the events of the morning after their night together. Perhaps the abhorrence she'd glimpsed during their fraught exchange, the deep trepidation that what had happened between them had been life-altering, and the long months following when a peculiar ache had lodged itself in her chest every time his name had crossed her mind, had all been in her overblown imagination.

Javier had moved on to other conquests, and had continued to aggressively pursue his *work hard, party harder* lifestyle if his presence in the tabloids was any indication.

So maybe her trepidation was for nothing, maybe she was just overthinking this—

'Do you intend to conduct the meeting standing up, Miss Nardozzi?'

Carla flinched and turned at the flat, detached tone.

Her breath locked in her lungs, every cell in her body clenching in freeze frame as she stared at the man sauntering down the side of the conference table.

In a dark grey pinstriped suit that accentuated his broad shoulders and a white shirt and navy tie that screamed understated elegance, Javier Santino didn't need the tough lawyers who flanked him to underscore his supremacy and importance. He was *still* hugely formidable and domineeringly sexy. His overpowering masculinity would continue to draw eyes to his sculptured cheekbones and uncharacteristically full mouth, which held a perpetual reddish tinge as if he'd been thoroughly and expertly kissed, long after he was well past his prime.

He stopped opposite her and, even across the vast polished surface, the sheer dominance of his aura slammed into her. Gold-flecked brown eyes pinned hers, one eyebrow lifted in cool, arrogant query.

Deep inside, past the numbness and the fear, something wild and hot and dangerous sparked to life, and she felt the ground shift beneath her feet.

She shouldn't have come... Then again, what choice did she have?

'Very well. I'll take that as a yes.' His gaze conducted an impersonal inspection of her face and body, then swung from her, releasing her from the disturbingly deep frisson that had taken hold of her. Striding to the head of the table, he pulled out a chair, unbuttoned his jacket in one deft move, and sat down. 'Since you also didn't answer my PA when she asked whether you wanted refreshments, I'll assume you don't want any?' Javier continued, the deep, smooth tenor of his voice igniting the flame higher.

Carla swung her head towards the departing PA, her mind unfreezing itself long enough to wonder how long she'd been caught in the dangerous tide of the past.

'No, I'm fine. Thank you.' She raised her voice slightly to catch Javier's PA. The woman turned and nodded with a cool smile before leaving the room.

'Good. Shall we begin?'

The magnetism that had gripped her outside as she'd stared at Javier's building returned full force. Her gaze returned to him, her heart beating faster as she stared at him.

There was no trace of the censure she'd expected, no hot-blooded Latin lip curl or even a hint of the fact that this man had seen her naked once, had done things to her body that still had the power to make her blood pound hot and hard through her veins.

He was going for impersonal. Stony. Businesslike.

As she shakily pulled out the chair he indicated to his right and sat down, Carla told herself it was okay to breathe in relief.

If Javier wanted to proceed with no acknowledgement of their past, then so would she. In fact, it was a brilliant thing. No need for further angst.

'I believe everything's been settled between our lawyers? You're finally willing to agree to the quarterly payment terms and the performance-related incentives stipulated in the contract, correct?'

Carla dragged her eyes from Javier to glance at her father. She spied the haughty desperation there, the silent command that their dirty laundry not be aired. She wanted to rail at him, demand to know what had possessed him to gamble away all her money, to jeopardise everything she'd worked for and bring her to the brink of bankruptcy. She didn't doubt that he'd have another blithe explanation, the callous hauteur he'd often displayed towards her as a child their only means of communication nowadays.

She glanced away again, deliberately numbing herself to the pain and disappointment. Steeling herself, she focused on Javier once more.

'Yes, I agree to your terms.'

'Unless, of course, there's any way you'd reconsider a larger, upfront payment?' her father suggested, squaring his shoulders as he planted his elbows on the table.

Javier's gaze didn't shift from her face. 'No. If you came here under the pretext of signing the final agreement only to try and renegotiate the terms, then you've wasted all of our time. I sincerely hope that's not the case, Miss Nardozzi.' The cold edge in his tone matched the look in his eyes.

Another shiver rippled over her. 'No, the clauses agreed upon are fine.'

Her father exhaled. 'Carla—'

'*Everything* is fine.' She struggled to keep her voice from wobbling through the lie as tension escalated in the room. 'Can we get on with it, please?'

Javier's gaze sharpened. 'You understand that, due to the delay in getting this signed, the cooling-off period will no longer apply? This contract, once signed, will be final and binding.'

Her fingers started to curl into her palms. Inhaling deeply, she placed them on the cool surface of the table and strove for composure. 'Yes. I really don't see why we're going over this again. My lawyers have explained everything to me. I'm ready to sign your document. All I need, Mr Santino, is a pen.'

If she'd been expecting a reaction, Carla realised she would be sorely disappointed. His gaze flicked with almost cruel lack of interest from her to his lawyers. An imperious nod, and the documents were produced and laid out before them. An elegant ball pen bearing his name arrived before her.

Shakily, she picked it up, signed and countersigned where indicated. The contracts were witnessed and exchanged. And her fate was sealed.

She would become the exclusive face of carefully selected J Santino products, called upon for advertising campaigns and publicity events whenever he chose.

It was done. With any luck, she could now negotiate further time with the bank back in Tuscany and save her family home. Not that it'd ever been a real home. These days it was more a showpiece property for her father to bask in the success he claimed she wouldn't have achieved without him.

But it was the only remaining roof over her head. The New York condo was gone, as was the chalet in Switzerland. *Everything* was gone.

Carla set the pen down and stood. 'Thank you for your time, Mr Santino. Now if you'll excuse us—'

'You're not free to go just yet, Miss Nardozzi.'

Her breath stumbled as Javier rose with fluid grace.

She stared up at him, meeting that stony expression once more. 'What…what more could we possibly have to discuss?'

A tight smile pursed his lips. 'It's confidential. Come into my office.' His gaze flicked over the table's occupants in a dismissive glance. 'Alone.'

Without waiting for a response, he headed for a set of double doors opposite from where she'd entered.

Her palms grew hot and she fought the urge to rub them against her thighs. Every instinct screamed at her to get up and walk out. She'd made it this far relatively unscathed. She'd seen Javier again, withstood his imposing presence, heard his voice, inhaled that singularly unique scent without losing her composure. What she'd dreaded most was over.

Yet she couldn't move.

'Now, Miss Nardozzi,' Javier insisted in cutting tones.

The atmosphere shifted again, men in expensive suits fidgeting beneath ricocheting tension.

'Carla,' her father's warning tone rumbled over her.

She ignored him, looking past him to the doors that led to freedom. Could Javier stop her from leaving? From re-treating back to that numb place where she was marginally cocooned from pain and betrayal?

Yes. Because she was now bound to him, a contracted employee who couldn't refuse *reasonable* requests.

Swallowing the hysterical laugh that rose in her throat, she stood, ignoring the collective muted sighs of relief that floated round the table.

Carla entered Javier's office and drew to a stunned stop. Unlike the rest of his company's workspace, this was an un-apologetically masculine domain. From the massive walnut desk and throne-like armchair set back against a solid wall, to the studded black sofas grouped around a glass and gold TV and entertainment centre on one side, the space shrieked a dominance that made her flesh tighten with acute premo-nition.

But no.

So far Javier had been cold and brutally businesslike. Uninterested in her, other than as another financial asset for his company. She had nothing to fear.

Behind her the door swung shut, followed by another distinct click.

Her gaze flew to Javier, to the tiny remote in his hand. A second later, he flung the control away, then advanced towards her with slow, precise strides. Her breath uselessly trapped in her lungs, Carla tilted her head to meet his gaze and the blood rushed from her head in a dizzying surge.

Because those mesmeric eyes were no longer cold. No longer impersonal. A very specific, very dangerous light blazed in their depths. A light that threatened to stop her heart altogether.

'At long last, here you are,' he murmured.

The savouring, triumphant statement made every nerve in her body jump.

'Here I am? What does that mean?' she retorted, fully aware her voice was bled of any power.

He stepped closer, amplifying his power and might by a thousand degrees. 'It means I never thought this day would arrive. You won't believe how many times I nearly threw in the towel. But revenge is a dish best served cold. Isn't that what they say?'

Ice filled her veins. *'Revenge?'*

He bent his head closer, as if sharing a salacious secret. 'Luckily, I'm a very patient man,' he whispered. 'I knew, sooner or later, I could count on you and your father's greed to bring you back to the contract table.'

Carla's mouth dropped open, her heart falling to her toes. *'Dio mio.'* Her voice snagged on the words.

He leaned back and smiled. A pure evil smile that drew her dumbfounded gaze to his sensual lips. '*Sí, this* is the expression I've been waiting three years for.'

He'd been scheming. Laying the perfect bait for her

downfall. And like a lamb to the slaughter, she'd walked right into his trap.

Just as she'd been a weak, trusting lamb throughout her father's machinations, childhood fears of abandonment unconsciously stalking her into adulthood so stealthily that she hadn't realised she was being taken advantage of until it was too late. She'd sacrificed herself for her father.

And now she was to be a sacrifice for Javier Santino.

A sheer wall of dread rose before her, every single brain cell frozen as she was caught in suspended animation.

From far away, she heard Javier speak but she couldn't rouse herself from the horror of her circumstances.

Firm hands caught her elbows. Eyes fringed by thick lashes narrowed. 'What is wrong with you, Carla? Or should I call you The Ice Princess? Isn't that what the media calls you? You're certainly dressed for it.'

Numbly, she glanced down at her white palazzo pantsuit. The jacket's severely cut style opened at the elbows when she lifted her arms, and the sleeves dropped almost to the floor. Teamed with a white silk camisole and white stilettos, the ensemble broadcasted a cutting-edge style suitable for a woman at the top of her game. Or so the stylist had insisted when she'd arrived with the clothes this morning. Staring at the get-up, she suddenly saw differently.

White, for innocent sacrificial lambs.

White, for fools.

The hysterical laughter she'd tried to stem bubbled up from her chest and burst free. It sounded strange in the impressive, masculine room. But the crack in her self-control felt good.

So good she couldn't stop laughing.

Javier blinked, then jerked her once. 'Carla!'

Laughter cut off like a light switch. 'I thought I was only Miss Nardozzi to you?'

Puzzlement tracked over his face. 'What's wrong with you?' he demanded again.

'What do you care?' she flung at him.

'I don't, except I'd prefer not to have a conversation with a woman who's acting like a walking, talking zombie.'

'Right in this moment, I wish I were one.'

A dark frown clamped his brow. 'Excuse me?'

Another bubble of laughter bursting free, she shook her head. 'You should see your face, Javier. Is this not going how you expected? Did you expect me to be a quivering idiot in the light of your revelation? Did you—*what are you doing*?' she screeched as strong arms lifted her off her feet.

In half a dozen strides he pinned her against a wall. They stared at each other for a charged, timeless second. Then someone moved. Her gasp was swallowed by the mouth that slanted over hers, the domineering possession so electrifyingly potent, every trace of numbness was instantly zapped from her body.

In its place raw, intense emotion flooded. Every sensation she'd retreated from surged in a tidal wave of feeling, concentrating in that powerful connection of their fused lips. From one heartbeat to the next, they tore at each other. Tongues duelled, groans fought for supremacy, hands searched and groped. And Javier came out on top each time, his indomitable will pounding into her, into the kiss until she was a seething ball of sensation, ready to be done with as he pleased.

Gradually the other emotions receded, leaving her with a deep, decadent arousal she'd only believed existed in her dreams. The realisation that it did not had her surging up on tiptoes, eager to experience more of it.

Javier deepened the kiss, his hands moulding her, his teeth nipping at her full lower lip. Powerful thighs parted hers and he planted himself firmly between them, the evidence of his arousal unmistakeable.

Dio, but he felt glorious. And he made her feel *alive*!

About to spike her hand through his hair, demand more, more, *more*, she was brought back to earth when her arms were wrenched from around his neck and pinned ruthlessly to her sides.

'Do I have your attention now?' he rasped.

White lamb. Sacrificial fool.

She glimpsed the menacing look in his eyes and her insides turned to useless jelly. 'Wh-what do you plan to do to me?'

Teeth bared in a cruel smile, he dropped his head and rubbed the tip of his nose against hers in a gesture so divorced from affection, it staked a cold knife of fear in her heart.

'Where would be the fun in laying it all out for you, Principessa? All you need to know is that by the time I'm done with you, you'll know that you should never have used me the way you did three years ago. Before I'm done with you, Carla Nardozzi, you'll get on your knees and beg my forgiveness.'

CHAPTER ONE

One month later

'SIR, I THINK you'll want to turn on the TV.'

'And why would I want to do that?' Javier Santino drawled, not lifting his head from the graphics spread on his desk. His designers had done an exemplary job, the sample bottles for the launch of his new and exclusive tequila line truly exquisite.

About to reach for the glossy image he'd settled on, he paused when his PA rushed to the far side of the room and grabbed the remote.

Javier sighed. Had she not been ruthlessly efficient, he wouldn't have forgiven her occasional bouts of excitable behaviour. Making a mental note to crush that tiny irregularity out of her, he turned from the view of Manhattan spread beyond his corner-office window and watched her flick on the TV.

'You asked the PR department to alert you if and when any of our clients make the news. They just called. Carla Nardozzi is on every channel.'

Javier froze.

In all his nearly thirty-three years, only two names had possessed the power to stop his breath. For the first three decades of his life, it'd been his father's name. The day after his thirtieth birthday, Carla Nardozzi's had joined the list. Both names sent icy chills of rage down his spine. Both robbed him of the ability to speak.

Three years after the event, his brief dalliance with Carla and how it'd ended still stuck between his ribs like the sharpest stiletto. As much as he detested himself for his weakness, he'd never been able to put it behind him.

It didn't matter that he knew why. The fact that he'd been unable to do anything about it angered him even more. In the grand scheme of things, Carla Nardozzi should be forgettable. A blip in his memory that shouldn't be worth his time or effort.

And yet all efforts to consign her to the *ex to forget* pile had been fruitless. He'd even gone as far as to pull her further into his orbit, just so he could tackle this particular thorn in his side once and for all.

'That will be all, Shannon,' he forced out, his gaze on the pictures flickering on the muted screen. He didn't recognise the building the paparazzi were crowded in front of, but the medical vehicles flashing past had him striding across the room.

His PA's retreat barely registered as Javier activated the sound.

'Miss Nardozzi's condition has now been downgraded from critical to serious but stable. Doctors are monitoring her closely following her awakening from her brief medically induced coma and she's responding well to treatment at this top medical facility in Rome.

'To recap events, Carla Nardozzi was airlifted from her father's estate and training facility in Tuscany following a fall during training. Unconfirmed allegations suggest the world number one figure skater's trainer, Tyson Blackwell, is being questioned by authorities following the accident...'

Javier flung the remote down. 'Shannon!'

The door opened a second later. 'Yes, sir?'

'Tell my pilot to ready my jet. We leave for Rome immediately.'

'Of course.'

Before the door had shut, he was picking up his phone. He knew the number by heart, although these days his dealings with Draco Angelis were more business than pleasure. The reason for it pierced another jagged blade of anger through him. Javier gritted his teeth as he pressed the receiver to his ear.

'You've heard the news,' the deep voice rumbled.

'When did this happen and why wasn't I informed immediately?' Javier snapped.

'Cool it, *amigo*. I've had my hands a little full on this side of town,' Draco responded.

Javier's ire didn't abate. 'You have people in place to ensure the right parties know what's going on. I should be at the top of your list of people to communicate with when it comes to Carla Nardozzi.'

A brief, pregnant pause. 'Agreed. You would've been informed before the hour was out. You just beat me to it.'

'For the sake of our continued working relationship, I'll choose to believe that.'

Draco exhaled. 'Is there anything else going on here I should know about, Santino?'

Javier reined himself in with effort, tightening his control on the emotions rumbling beneath his skin. This was business. Nothing else. 'Aside from the fact that I've invested several million dollars in your client and am about to invest several more? You think I should have to find out about her accident from the media? I don't appreciate being placed in a position where I'm caught unawares by situations like these.'

A deep sigh echoed down the line, and Javier got the impression that the formidable Draco Angelis had something on his mind. 'Point taken.'

'When did all this happen?' Javier was aware of the distinct bite to his voice but he didn't soften his tone. Any hint of softness was seen as a sign of weakness. And he'd sworn an oath a very long time ago never to be seen as weak or gullible.

'Yesterday.'

'And this induced coma?' he pressed.

'It was only overnight until they were sure there wasn't any brain damage. She's awake and the doctors are optimistic she's out of the woods.'

Javier exhaled. He released his death grip on his phone when the plastic creaked. 'I should be wheels up in an hour but I'd appreciate frequent updates on her condition.'

'You're coming to Italy?' Draco's voice expressed surprise.

Javier snapped up his briefcase shut and headed for the door. 'Considering how much I've invested in our mutual client, I believe a personal interest in her recovery is well within my rights. I'll see you in seven hours.'

He hung up and walked past his PA's desk.

'Cancel all my appointments until further notice.'

She opened her mouth then immediately shut it.

In his limo minutes later, he tried to wrestle his fury under control.

So what if Carla Nardozzi had rejected him in a way only the father who'd barely acknowledged his existence had done? After years of biding his time, he'd finally found a way to get his own back. The Ice Princess would be taught a salutary lesson. All he needed was to ensure she got back on her feet in order for him to deliver the punishment she truly deserved.

His emotions had nothing to do with this.

This was a matter of business. And of his pride.

Nothing else.

Carla tried to lift her head off the pillow and was immediately engulfed in a fog of pain and confusion.

'No, *signorina*, don't try and move.'

She relaxed, and the pain receded a touch. But the confusion remained. She'd been sure she was dreaming. And yet the voices and images flitting through her mind had been so vivid, so real.

Her father's voice had been unmistakeable. He'd been there the few times she'd woken up in the strange, sterile room.

But it was the other, deeper voice she'd heard the last time she'd woken that confused her and made her heart race. The change in the lighting suggested she'd fallen asleep some time after hearing *him*.

By all accounts that voice didn't belong here...wherever this cold, grey *here* was.

The last time they'd met, he'd been icily indifferent, a ruthless businessman intent on one thing—getting her to sign along the dotted line.

Or at least, he had been...until he'd had her exactly where he wanted her. Until that kiss.

Like a blurred lens swinging into sharp focus, the memory of the kiss burned bright and insistent. Along with the recollection of the way he'd looked at her afterward.

Javier Santino had looked at her with pure hatred. And she didn't blame him. After what she'd done three years ago, he had every right to detest her. It didn't help that her will power withered away to nothing in his presence. But since that unfortunate day a month ago, she'd summoned enough strength to assure herself nothing would happen.

Javier hated her. She'd dealt his ego a great blow. And a ruthlessly powerful and charismatic man like that would never forget an insult to his pride.

Which bemused her as to why he'd kissed her in the first place.

Or had she kissed him...?

Memory blurred and confusion remounted. Carla lifted her hand to her head. Tracing her fingers gingerly over a particularly sore spot, she gasped as pain ricocheted through her. A dull throb in her other wrist brought her attention to the fact that it was in a cast.

'Where am I?' she attempted, swallowing painfully around a dry throat.

The buxom woman bustling around her paused and Carla noticed her nurse's uniform for the first time. 'In a private hospital in Roma,' she replied, smiling her sympathy. 'You suffered a bad fall and a particularly nasty concussion.'

Of course. Memories of her accident resurged. The row with her father. Then with her trainer, Tyson Blackwell. Her instincts screaming at her in the moments before the accident to walk away. Then the sickening twist and the ice rushing towards her, one arm out in front of her in a vain attempt to break her fall.

She curled her fist and rested it in her lap. 'How long have I been here?'

'Three days. You've been asleep for most of the time since you came out of surgery, but it's great that you're healthy. You'll be on the mend soon. I'll get the doctor now, then you can visit with your family. They've been quite anxious to see you awake.'

'They?' she echoed, puzzled. Her father was her only family. Had been since… Carla swallowed as tears pierced her eyelids, surprising her.

She hadn't cried since that fateful night when she was ten years old. She'd known then that tears would earn her nothing but a sharp tongue and dire punishment and had quickly wised up.

'*Sì,*' the nurse responded. 'Your *papà* has been here throughout. He left about an hour ago, just before your young man arrived. *He's* been haunting the halls ever since his arrival.' The older woman cast her a sly glance. 'You're lucky to have such a passionate man in your life.'

'I…what…?'

The nurse patted her hand. 'Don't fret. The doctor will be here soon.' She exited, leaving Carla in a deeper state of confusion than before.

Pull yourself together.

Grabbing the remote that adjusted the bed, Carla slowly raised herself up, just as the doctor arrived.

'Signorina Nardozzi, it's good to see you awake.'

Carla nodded a reply, then lay there patiently as she was checked over, the fog clearing with each passing second, and with it a heart heavy with foreboding and regret.

The accident had happened because she'd been fleeing her demons. Pushing herself beyond her endurance in light of what her father had done and their ongoing rowing. Finally understanding why he'd been even more callously demanding these past few months had done nothing to alleviate the pain lodged beneath her breast.

She had well and truly reached a crossroads with her father.

Carla forced herself to listen to the doctor's prognosis. The state of her health was directly connected to her career. Despite the changes she intended to make, she needed to ensure her health remained optimal. The very roof over her head was dependent on it.

'Your father mentioned you're eager to return to training?' the doctor disclosed once he'd reeled out his list of dos and don'ts. 'Your next figure-skating event is in two months, I believe?'

'Yes,' she replied. It wasn't a championship event, but an important one nonetheless.

The portly man frowned. 'I advise against any form of training for a few weeks. Two weeks of total rest if you heal fast enough. Four weeks just to be on the safe side before you begin any strenuous exercise. Your wrist on the other hand will need a little longer than that.'

'What about publicity work—photo shoots and such? I have commitments to fulfil.' Her contract with J Santino Inc. didn't include lying about in hospital beds. She was surprised Javier hadn't sent his lawyers after her already considering the stringent clauses in her contract.

The doctor's frown deepened. 'I strongly recommend that

you take at least two weeks without any stress on your body. After that, perhaps if you agree to engage private care—'

Carla shook her head. 'That won't be necessary. I can take care of myself—'

'She'll have private care from the day she's released. You have my word on that, Doctor.'

Carla's breath caught in her throat at the deep voice that preceded the sleek, powerfully built man who entered the room.

So…she hadn't been dreaming after all.

Javier approached. From the top of his dark wavy hair to the tip of his handmade designer shoes, he commanded a formidable, absorbing presence that reduced the rest of the room's occupants to mere spectators as his intense, dark brown eyes locked on her.

Tongue-tied, she watched him approach with measured, self-assured strides until his broad shoulders filled her vision.

'What are you doing here?' Her vocal cords, rough from disuse, rasped the words.

Javier's eyebrows arched, his gaze cuttingly cynical. 'News of your terrible accident has been all over the media. Your adoring fans are camped outside the hospital. You think me so uncaring that I would stay away at a time like this?'

His voice was smooth. Deep and warm and beautifully nuanced with inflections from his Spanish mother tongue. Mesmerising enough to disguise the vein of cruel cynicism to anyone but her.

Carla heard it loud and clear. It cut right to the heart of her. But she refused to look away. Whatever Javier intended for her—he'd spent the better part of a year dangling the lucrative sponsorship carrot in front of her father just so he could get to her, after all—she would face it head-on. She'd spent far too long bowing her head down. It might have taken her the best part of twenty-four years to stand up for herself. But she was done taking orders from anybody. A part of her regretted that it had taken this long, that her actions might have caused ripples she'd never be able to reverse, but it was better late than never.

'Thank you for your concern, but, as you can see, I'm in private consultation with my doctor, so if you'd excuse me?'

A nervous throat cleared. 'I'm sorry, *signorina*, but I understood from your father that Mr Santino was permitted to be here,' the doctor offered.

She forced her gaze to remain on Javier's. 'The permission wasn't my father's to give.'

Tense silence descended on the room. Javier's eyes gleamed, an almost unholy relish in the mahogany depths before one corner of his mouth lifted. 'Are you suggesting the doctor throw me out, Carla? Or are you not up to dealing with me right now?'

Her stomach hollowed, the unspoken threat in the words gnawing at her. 'I'm up to dealing with anything. I just don't think this is the right time or place. Perhaps you could come back later.' Or never.

His jaw flexed. 'I could, but why bother? I think what the doctor was trying to say was that you need further rest when you leave here. In light of what's happened, I'm prepared to suspend any commitments to J Santino Inc. until you're well enough to commence your sponsorship duties. You'll also have round-the-clock care by medical professionals.'

The doctor nodded eagerly. 'That's a very wise decision—'

'That's very generous of you, but I won't be needing your help with my recuperation,' she bit out, hiding her shock that Javier would be prepared to go to such lengths to help her recovery. She didn't doubt he had his motives for his overt generosity, but they were none she intended to subject herself to.

She held her breath as he moved closer to the bed. She was forced to tilt her head up to look at him; her head swam as the magnitude of his persona hit her full force.

'You may have forgotten the small print in the contract you signed, Carla, so I'll refresh your memory. It included my company, and therefore me, being made aware of and taking steps to ameliorate any new medical issues that might adversely affect our agreement. You being out of commission for several weeks has the potential to reflect badly on our association. Unless I choose to be…magnanimous.'

Carla managed to pry her gaze from the sensual mouth that dripped poison onto her skin. 'I'm sorry that my accident inconveniences you.'

'It's unfortunate, yes, but I'm willing to work with you provided you don't resort to stubbornness. Or perhaps you wish me to get my lawyers to pry that information from the hospital administrators?'

'How dare you?' she breathed.

Javier's narrow-eyed gaze flicked to the doctor and nurse who watched them with unabashed curiosity. 'If you've finished, Doctor, perhaps I can speak to Miss Nardozzi in private? You have my assurance that we'll reach agreement about the best way forward for her aftercare.'

Carla's heart climbed into her throat as the doctor nodded almost reverently before leaving, trailed by the nurse, who most unwillingly pried her eyes from Javier's body.

The moment the door shut behind them, the private hospital room shrank. Every inch of her focus zeroed in on the man who stood watching her in utter, dread-inducing silence, dark eyes piercingly intense.

Slowly, inexorably, his gaze wandered over her, lingering in places that made her breath catch.

She became hyperaware of the thin, insubstantial hospital gown and blanket that covered her body. The almost debilitating weakness in her limbs that had nothing to do with her health and everything to do with how this man made her feel just by being in the same room as her.

It'd been that way from the moment they met, three years ago, in Miami. The weekend from hell was firmly engraved in her mind. A naive twenty-one-year-old, striking out against the rigours that battened her down. A dangerously captivating man who'd represented the exact opposite of the caution she should've exercised that night, he'd been like a blazing comet in her dark world.

Except with morning had come the brutal realisation that she'd risked much more than her independence.

'Suddenly you have nothing to say?'

'I have plenty to say,' she rasped through a painful throat. 'But you seem to be in the mood to throw your weight about. I thought I'd just wait until you tire yourself out.'

A grim smile chased across his lips. 'Have you forgotten, *cara*? I don't tire very easily. Especially when it comes to the things I'm passionate about.'

Raw heat replaced the weakness in her limbs, firing her blood and making her head pound.

He advanced a few final steps, and stared down at her. Then he reached for the water jug on her bedside table. Still keeping his eyes on her, he poured a glass of water, inserted a handy straw and held it to her lips.

'Drink.'

She wanted to refuse. But her throat hurt. She was beyond thirsty. And getting back on her feet as quickly as possible was imperative. She couldn't begin to take control of her life from a hospital bed.

She dropped her gaze from his imperious regard, and parted her lips. Sucking on the straw, she drew the cool water into her mouth and shuddered with relief as the soothing liquid assuaged her ravaged throat.

He let her draw another mouthful, then he pulled the straw away. 'Take it easy, you don't want to make yourself ill again.'

The sound that emerged from her throat felt blissfully less abrasive. 'Your audience is gone. Please stop pretending you care about my health.'

He returned the glass to the nightstand. 'The state of

your health is directly connected to the millions I stand to lose if you don't meet the terms of your contract. Trust me, there's no pretence on my part. Tell me what happened with your trainer.'

Carla frowned as the unwanted memory sliced across her thoughts. She'd let her emotions get the better of her. Had refused to listen to her instincts even though she'd known training with Tyson Blackwell had been a mistake. Hell, her agent and friend, Draco, had warned her repeatedly about Blackwell.

Further regret made her purse her lips. 'He was a mistake that never should've happened.'

The moment the words left her lips, she felt the blood drain from her face. It took a single glance at Javier to see that he was just as affected by the words.

They were almost identical to what she'd said to him three years ago. The dark curl of his unbelievably sensual lips condemned her poor choice of words.

'I… I meant—'

'I'm well aware of what you meant. You seem to make a habit of collecting and leaving a trail of mistakes in your wake. You asked me what I was doing here. It's quite simple, *querida*. It's time to honour the promise I made to you a month ago.'

CHAPTER TWO

Carla's stomach hollowed. 'What is that supposed to mean?'

He didn't answer for a minute. Instead, he strolled to the single window that let in bright sunlight, glanced out for a moment, then turned.

If anything, his silhouette was even more formidable, his almost god-like stature drawing her gaze to his captivating frame.

'The reason you were chosen to be the face of the J Santino luxury line was because you're an expert at blending the illusion of innocence with ruthless ambition.'

'If there's a compliment in there you expect me to thank you for, I'll need a moment or two to think about it,' she replied.

The haloed outline of his shoulders lifted in a shrug. 'The results speak for themselves. Or at least they used to.'

'Is there a point to all this?'

'Your choices lately have been…disappointing, to say the least.'

'My choices?'

'You dragged out your negotiations with Draco Angelis's agency until he threatened to walk away. I'm guessing you realised, almost too late, that playing hard to get with him would get you nowhere? Then you insisted on associating yourself with a trainer whose reputation should've made you stay well clear of him.'

Carla swallowed hard against the need to tell him why. But she could see no way to set the record straight without pointing a direct finger at her father. And in a way, hadn't she also been at fault for desperately clinging to a familial bond that was only in her mind? 'My last trainer retired. Tyson Blackwell was only supposed to be temporary—'

'He was known to push his trainees too hard. You should've had nothing to do with him,' he cut across her.

Her breath shuddered out. 'I didn't want to. My father made a deal with him without my knowledge,' she muttered.

Disapproval vibrated off him. 'Then you should've hired someone else.'

She wanted to blurt out that she'd said the same thing to her father, instigating yet another row. A row during which she'd discovered she had no choice but to work with Blackwell because there was no money to hire anyone else. A row that set in motion a series of disagreements that still remained unresolved. Ones she wouldn't be able to brush under the carpet this time, even though it meant facing the hard truth—that her father loved the prestige and financial reward she brought him much more than he loved her.

Staunching the anguish before it bled into her voice, she replied, 'We both know why you pursued me to sign with you. So why are we having this conversation?'

'Because aside from our impending *private* matters, your father made an excellent case on your behalf by convincing me you were a good bet.'

'Wasn't it the other way round? Didn't you pursue him because you convinced him you were a good bet for my image?'

'Is that what he told you?' he enquired silkily, his tone taunting.

She pursed her lips and glanced away. When her fingernails cut into her palm, she forced herself to relax her fist. For the past few months, ever since she had broached the subject of untangling her father from his active role as her manager, their relationship had grown more strained than ever. Tensions had increased until an argument last month when he'd branded her ungrateful and irresponsible. Carla hadn't fooled herself into thinking the haggard look her father had worn in the past few weeks had anything to do with familial concern for her well-being. Time and hard lessons had taught her otherwise. But she hadn't known the reason behind her father's almost visceral reaction to her wanting to take a different path in her career. Not until six weeks ago, after the lavish charity event he'd given in their home in Tuscany. A weekend where her eyes had been opened in more ways than one.

Carla steeled her heart against the pain she'd never managed to suppress. Appearances were everything to Olivio Nardozzi, enough for her to know she was nothing but a meal ticket to the man who had raised her. Any threat to the lifestyle her father believed was owed to him had been disposed of with ruthless efficiency the moment Olivio became aware of his daughter's exceptional talent.

It was the reason her father had relinquished control to her when she'd come of age, but had legally tied up his role in her career as her manager. Twenty-one and reeling from her mother's sudden death, she'd fooled herself into thinking that the working collaboration with her father would ease a relationship whose foundations had been decimated when her mother had walked out on them both when Carla was ten.

With the passage of time, Carla had been prepared to forgive the fact that he'd chosen to tie her in knots professionally at the moment when she'd been most vulnerable. She'd chosen to believe that, somewhere deep down, her father had loved her mother and was reacting just as strongly to her death. What she couldn't forgive was her father cunningly plotting three years later to cement a lucrative business association by attempting to marry her off to Draco Angelis.

Willing calm into her body, she lifted her gaze as Javier paced closer. 'So you're here to do what exactly? Ensure I toe some sort of line set by you?'

'Among other things, I intend to ensure this...' he touched a hand to the wound dressing above her right temple '...

and this...' a drift of his fingers over her cast-bound wrist '...don't happen again.'

Carla gritted her teeth against the heat dredging through her. On top of everything else, she didn't need the reminder that this man's touch elicited the most decadent sensation inside her. She jerked her arm away, hiding the twinge of pain in her wrist. 'Please don't touch me.'

His fist balled for an unguarded second before he dropped his hand. She didn't need to look up to know she'd succeeded in angering him further. 'Your co-operation in seeing to your own health would help matters proceed smoothly. And please look at me when I'm talking to you.'

A childish urge to refuse surfaced. Reluctantly she raised her gaze, squashing the electricity that fizzed through her when his eyes locked on her. 'As I told you, I'm perfectly capable of taking care of myself. Once I'm back home in Tuscany—'

'You're not returning home.'

She frowned. 'Of course I am. It's my home.' Albeit a home that felt more like a museum and her father's way of congratulating himself for what *she'd* achieved. But it was the only home she had left, and the only thing standing between her and losing *that* home was her contract with Javier.

'In Tuscany, the nearest adequate medical facility should you need one is over sixty miles away. You were lucky this time that there was an air ambulance nearby when you fell. Tempting fate again is unwise. Besides, I want you where I can keep an eye on you.'

'Fine, I'll stay here in Rome. I can rent an apartment here—' She stopped speaking when he shook his head.

'No. New York or Miami is a much better option.'

'For you, you mean?'

'Of course. As much as I love your fair city, I have an important launch in a few weeks that needs my attention. I can't hop on a plane whenever you make an unfortunate choice. Besides, you were contracted to be in New York for your sponsorship duties sooner rather than later. And before you trot out an excuse about talking to your father, I already have. He's agreed.'

Bitterness dredged her insides. As much as she wanted to vocally condemn her father, she kept her mouth shut. Doing so would only hand Javier further ammunition against her. She would deal with her father later. 'So do all your clients get this special attention from you?'

'No, *querida*, I reserve this for ice princesses who believe they're above the mores that govern normal human beings,' he drawled.

'I don't—'

'Save the denial. I have first-hand experience of the way you operate, remember?'

The accusation stung deep. Licking dry lips, she shook her head. 'That was a long time ago, Javier. What happened three years ago...that wasn't me... I shouldn't have—'

His hiss of anger stopped her words. 'Stop before you dig yourself in deeper. Our association only requires you to recite rehearsed lines and act as if every J Santino product you endorse is as essential to you as the air you breathe. And when you're healthy enough, that is exactly what you'll do. In the meantime, keep pretending you're the perfect creature the public perceives you to be. But when we're in private, do me a favour and spare me the lies. I find it demeaning and frankly embarrassing.'

The rock that had lodged itself in her throat with each harsh word from his lips almost prevented her from speaking. 'Is your ego so badly bruised that you can't put what happened between us behind you? And don't pretend you're here just to protect your investment. You have over a thousand employees and a team of lawyers who could've relayed your instructions as effectively as you. You didn't need to fly all this way just to...'

'Just to what?' he invited smoothly, his tone almost bored as he flicked a non-existent speck off his sleeve.

'Can you tell me honestly that you don't want to make me suffer for being the only woman who didn't fall for Javier Santino's world-renowned machismo?'

A careless shrug. 'Why would I be bothered about machismo when you fell so readily for something far more... earthy? Much more satisfying?' he taunted.

Her face flamed, memories she couldn't stem rushing to the fore. 'If it was so satisfying, then why do you hate me so much?' she blurted before she could stop herself. Carla berated herself for asking so obvious a question. She knew why he hated her. Still on shaky ground after her first full-on rebellion against her father, she'd fallen headlong into Javier's arms. Only what she'd imagined would be a casual encounter had been *much more*. So much more that she'd been reeling the morning after, desperately aware that what had happened between them was in no way a casual fling. She'd deliberately stricken the heart of his pride, the almost self-destructive trajectory she'd set herself on seemingly impossible to veer from. It wasn't a moment she'd been proud of.

'Hate is a useless emotion, one I don't waste my time practising. Self-respect on the other hand, especially when it reflects on my reputation, is of paramount importance to me.'

She frowned. 'What are you talking about?'

'You may have the public fooled, *chiquita*, but we both know you have no shame. Throwing yourself at a man who doesn't want you is one thing. Throwing yourself at a man who is engaged to another woman is a different matter entirely. I didn't delegate this trip because you need to be made aware of the consequences of a scandal should you choose to be so unwise as to keep pursuing Angelis.'

Carla flinched. 'Draco? I'm not pursuing him. I haven't done anything wrong...' She trailed off, the look on Javier's face inviting her to not bother.

'Are you implying that the pictures of you on social media

actively throwing yourself at him at your father's charity event six weeks ago were fake?'

Flames of guilt lit her insides. 'It wasn't what it looked like…it didn't mean anything.' Draco Angelis was the brother of her best friend, Maria Angelis, and the big brother she'd never had. Sure, at one very brief point during her teenage years she'd fancied herself infatuated with him, and had even used him to protect herself against unwanted male advances a few times. Six weeks ago, with her budding re-solve to take a more active role in her life and career still shaky, she'd leant on him more than perhaps had been wise.

Luckily he'd understood and hadn't held her less than stellar behaviour against her, and neither had his fiancée, Rebel Daniels. Watching Javier's expression, she knew he wouldn't be as accommodating of her explanations.

'Things are never as they seem with you, are they?' he confirmed.

Suddenly weary, she sagged against the pillow, her head beginning to throb. 'Think what you will. I don't need to justify my private life to you. If you've finished saying what you came here to say, please leave.'

Silence greeted her response. She didn't need to look at him to know his gaze would be heavy with anger and con-demnation. 'Agree to return to New York with me and I will.'

'You make it sound as if I have a choice. Isn't this part of your grand revenge scheme?'

'Perhaps it is. But I'm happy to delay what comes next. As long as I get what I want.'

Carla sighed and squeezed her eyes shut. '*Sì*. You win. New York. Rome. I don't really care. Just leave me in peace for now, if you can bring yourself to.'

Javier stood looking down at her. The soft, delicate arch of her lashes fanned against her cheek as she kept her eyes closed. Her complexion was alarmingly pale, and he experi-enced a twinge of guilt for wearing her out when she needed to rest. A second later, he pushed the feeling away. He of all people knew just how Carla Nardozzi's outwardly delicate frame hid a core of icy steel. She hadn't risen to number one in her chosen profession by being a wilting flower, no matter how much she outwardly projected an air of shy, innocent fragility.

His jaw clenched as he recalled that her innocence had been real once upon a time. But it had been ruthlessly sacrificed on the altar of what she'd wanted more—the attention of Draco Angelis.

Some men collected virginities as trophies. He'd never been one of them. But his preference for a more experienced bed partner had abandoned him the moment he'd met Carla Nardozzi three years ago.

He gave a grim smile. A *lot* of things had abandoned him during those insane few weeks, including his common sense.

High from closing the deal of a lifetime that had seen him propelled into the echelons of *world richest* the week before his thirtieth birthday, he'd thrown a series of lavish parties in his homes across the world, the wildest and most decadent of which had culminated in Miami, the place he called his true home.

The place he'd experienced Carla.

Javier jerked himself from the memories. The reminder of the gullible idiot he'd been in the days following raked rough and jagged over his senses.

Never again.

It took several minutes to realise she wasn't deliberately ignoring him and feigning sleep. Carla had truly fallen asleep, her breathing soft but deep, the lines of exhaustion he hadn't wanted to acknowledge now smoothing out on her face.

He stepped back from the bed before another guilty twinge lanced him. He'd come to reiterate the message he'd delivered to her in his office a month ago. Standing there watching her sleep—her perfect face relaxed and enthralling—was an inane exercise.

About to turn away, he paused as a niggling thought impinged. It was the same sensation he'd experienced when she'd turned up in his New York office to sign the contract.

Despite her spirited words just now, an air of apathy surrounded her that seemed at variance with the woman whose ambition had made her competitors cow before her on the ice rink. Magnificence like that didn't happen overnight, and Carla Nardozzi was known for her indefatigable dedication to her discipline. And yet, she'd seemed a shadow of herself during their meeting in New York. It was that inkling of ennui he'd sensed that had propelled him to get a rise out of her...by kissing her.

It was what was stopping him leaving the room right now.

Having never experienced such an emotion, Javier wasn't sure how to deal with it. And not knowing how to deal with a problem wasn't a scenario he readily accepted.

He told himself it was the reason he was sitting in the armchair in the corner of the room, watching Carla sleep two hours later. After all, he was a firm believer in confronting an issue before it grew out of hand.

He'd confronted the man he'd been told was his father when he was seventeen. And again when his mother had died. Both times the results had been traumatic enough to fell a lesser man. He'd chosen to absorb the experiences as the hard lessons he'd needed to forge his path in life. So what if being termed a bastard by the man whose blood ran through his veins had left an imagined hole in Javier's life for a long time? He'd learned with time that he could live without the soft trappings of family and endless entanglements of relationships that were, more often than not, fraught and tedious. The ideal family life he'd envied from afar as a child had proved to be nothing more than a cluster of blood relations fighting over what remained of a once prestigious aristocratic name.

He'd achieved more in his lifetime than his so-called an-
cestors had managed in several generations.

But the rejection still hurt...

Javier shrugged tense shoulders, ferociously denying the
voice in his head, and looked up as Carla murmured in her
sleep.

Clinically, he examined her, forcing himself to assess
what had drawn him so inexorably to her. She certainly
wasn't his type. Slim and far too delicate where he preferred
his women curvy and vivacious.

Yet, from the first moment he'd laid eyes on her, he'd been
captivated by the combination of ethereal beauty that com-
prised silky caramel-streaked chocolate hair, vivid green
eyes and a figure that begged for masculine hands, *his* hands,
to mould and possess.

And despite everything that had happened—her delib-
erate, callous insults and her flaying rejection the morning
after their passionate night together—he couldn't help the
rush of heat to his groin as he lingered on her full mouth
and the steady rise and fall of her breasts.

He surged to his feet, disgusted with himself for ogling
a sick, bedridden woman.

But Carla Nardozzi wasn't just any woman. She epito-
mised the very thing that Javier had struggled all his life to
effectively deny.

She'd rejected him because he hadn't been *good enough*.
Not once, but twice, she'd looked upon him as if he hadn't
been worthy to address her.

The family he didn't want or need had been allowed to
get away with treating him like that.

She would not.

And before their association was over, he would make
sure she took back every dismissive word, every scathing
look and gesture she'd spurned him with.

CHAPTER THREE

Even before Carla came fully awake, she knew he was still there. His presence was too oppressive, too hyper-intense, to dismiss.

Thankfully, her headache had lessened, and, even though her broken wrist throbbed, Carla felt much better and in control of herself than she'd been a few hours ago.

So she opened her eyes, and glanced at the occupant of the armchair.

Javier was asleep.

That in itself was shocking enough to observe—the man was larger than life, a demigod who surely didn't require the rejuvenating needs of mere mortals. But it was the transformation that had overcome his face that made her eyes widen. That made her stare shamelessly.

His arms were flung over the sides of the chair, his long legs splayed in front of him. The position offered an unfettered view of the stunning landscape of his body. Powerful taut thighs tapered to lean hips and a trim waist before veering up to display a torso that would've made any athlete proud. His deep chest and broad shoulders rose and fell and his slightly relaxed jawline drew attention to the stubble that had grown in the hours he'd been here. Almost reluctantly, her gaze traced his face.

Sinfully gorgeous, Javier's features had always been a subject of acute fascination for her and this time was no exception, despite his less than formidable demeanour in repose.

Heat dragged low in her belly as she recalled what that mouth had done to her, what she'd begged him to do to her during that mad, reckless night in Miami.

He'd fulfilled her every wish, and more, with an intensity

that had sent her running for cover in a blind panic the next morning. Carla had known that Javier was bad news for her. His healthy sex life and reputation for strictly temporary liaisons with women hadn't been a secret. She'd known even before she woke up in his bed that it was only a matter of time before he notched her name on his bedpost and moved on. *Dio mio*, she'd barely kept up with him during their night of passion, her inexperience blazing through every fumbled kiss and caress that had made his sensual lips twitch with tender humour. But it was the risk to her own emotions that had finally sent her scurrying.

That had made her strike out before he'd got round to rejecting her first.

'You stare at me with such fascination, it's almost enough to make me forgot the horror on your face when you looked upon me once upon a time.'

She jumped, her mind dragging itself to the present and to the ragged contempt in his voice. She forced herself to meet Javier's gaze. 'It wasn't horror. At least not at you.'

One sleek eyebrow lifted. 'Is that supposed to make me feel better, *pequeña*? That you were horrified with yourself for choosing me to be the man you lost your innocence to?'

'Is there anything I can say that will make you stop condemning me for what I said the next morning?'

The gleam in his eyes slowly hardened to merciless chips. Still splayed out in indolent abandon, he linked his fingers over his washboard stomach. 'You told me sleeping with me was the worst mistake of your life. Of course with the benefit of hindsight I see that I was being used all along. But even if I hadn't believed you then or found a way to excuse that insult, your behaviour since has proven your words to be true. Why should I believe that anything you say now isn't just to save face?'

'Save face?' she said, confused.

'Angelis is engaged to another woman, is he not? He's

made his choice and it wasn't you. It's natural you wouldn't want the world to know how you truly feel about him.'

'I'm not in love with him. I'm really not,' she stressed when mocking disbelief draped his face.

'Then why were you seen kissing him at your charity event in Tuscany last month?'

'Would you believe me if I told you it was a mistake?'

He surged to his feet in one smooth bound, a volatile emotion bristling from his large frame. 'No. The fact is your obsession with him continues, and you don't seem to be interested in the small matter of him being committed to another. You just want what you want, don't you, Carla, and to hell with the consequences?'

'No, of course I don't. I'd never do that—'

'But you did.' He strolled closer, a predator stalking his prey, until he stood over her. 'The evidence speaks for itself.'

She shook her head, unable to believe she was having this conversation with Javier. 'It's obvious you've made up your mind about me. I said I'd return to New York with you. So why are you still here? I'm not exactly in the position to make a run for it.'

A dark frown clamped his brows. He shoved his hands in his pockets and shrugged. 'You fell asleep before I got your word that you'll stay away from Angelis from now on.'

Carla sat up gingerly and swung her legs over the side. The wave of dizziness that washed over her was blessedly brief. 'He's my agent. Avoiding him will be impossible. And counter-productive, don't you think?'

'You can and you will. Angelis has enough executives to ensure he has no personal dealings with you from now on. I'll contact him myself to make sure the request is understood.'

'Are you going to forbid me from letting him become my trainer too, which was his suggestion?' She shook her head. 'If I didn't know better, I'd think you were jealous. And you don't wear it particularly well.'

Deep, unamused laughter erupted from his throat, mocking her every word. 'Don't delude yourself. Scandal may sell newspapers, but my company has remained free of it up till now and I intend to ensure it stays that way. As for training you, we've agreed that it would be better if someone else assumes that role.'

Her unhurt hand gripped the side of the bed. 'You've been discussing me with Draco behind my back?'

'I've been trying to minimise the impact of what's happened—what are you doing? You shouldn't be on your feet.'

Carla swayed for a moment before she managed to steady herself. 'I should if I want to use the bathroom. Or are you going to forbid that too?'

A faint wash of colour highlighted his sculpted cheekbones and his lips pursed for a moment. 'Don't be ridiculous.'

She wanted to protest the ridiculousness of the whole situation. But she was too busy wincing as she placed her weight on her left foot. Too late, she remembered she'd landed hard on her hip. A second later, she was swung off her feet.

The shock of the sudden action halted her breath for a second before she regained her senses. 'What are you doing? Put me down!'

'No. You're in no fit state to be walking anywhere.'

He hoisted her up, his steps sure and confident as he strode into the adjoining bathroom. Painfully aware of her dishevelled state, she buried her reddening face in his chest. And was immediately bombarded with the unique, undeniably male scent of him. The urge to take greedy gulps of him assailed her, forcing her to do the opposite and hold her breath as he slowly lowered her to her feet.

Unable to stop herself, she risked a glance at him, to find his burnished bronze gaze on her.

'Umm…you can let me go now,' she ventured, her senses screaming at the electrifying grip he had on her arms.

He frowned. 'Will you be okay?' he asked brusquely. 'I'll go and get the nurse—'

'There's no need. I'll be fine.'

He stared at her for a few more seconds. Then he carefully stepped back. 'Don't lock the door,' he instructed.

Carla resisted the urge to perform an uncharacteristic eye roll. 'I'm not made of glass, Javier. I've suffered more falls in my career than most people will in a lifetime.'

If anything her answer drew an even deeper frown from him. 'Is that supposed to reassure me?'

'I wasn't aware that you needed my reassurance. Just my acquiescence to your every demand.'

His eyes darkened. 'You laid down the rules of our relationship, *querida*. Don't complain now that I'm playing by your standards.'

Carla was puzzling over that cryptic remark when he shut the door and left her in peace for the first time since waking up in hospital. She didn't doubt that she'd invited some degree of the hell Javier seemed intent on visiting upon her. But overall his actions pointed to a deeper reaction to what she'd done to warrant his almost volatile anger. Had she really bruised his ego that much? How could she have, when he'd been associated with some of the most captivatingly beautiful women in the world, both before and after their unfortunate one-night stand?

To complete her ablutions, she limped to the sink, washed up, and lifted her gaze to the mirror. With growing horror, she examined the bags under her eyes and the unkempt nest of her thick hair. She almost giggled hysterically at the thought of her father seeing her this way. For as long as she could remember, Olivio had demanded perfection in everything she did. She'd granted it. Because to do otherwise would've incurred his wrath. Besides, it'd been easier playing the perfect princess. It provided the flawless façade to hide behind. Seeking and attaining perfection meant she

didn't have to acknowledge the flawed individual behind
the mask.

Carla stared into the mirror, her heart thumping hard as
she acknowledged that the shell had well and truly cracked.
Her eyes looked bruised and haunted. But then what was
new? Pain and betrayal were effective tools in eroding any
chance of finding peace even while doing what one loved—

'Carla?'

The harsh rap of her name brought her up short. Quickly
running her fingers through her hair, she took a deep breath.
She would deal with her father and their acrimonious relationship once she got out of here.

First she needed to deal with the man intent on making
her pay dearly for her one monumental mistake.

The moment the doctor gave her the all-clear to leave later
that afternoon, Javier swung into action.

'Your father is having your things brought over. We'll
stay at my hotel tonight and fly out in the morning.'

She smoothed her hand over the dark orange dress and
matching shoes she'd found in her hospital closet. With the
help of the nurse, she'd taken a quick shower and pulled her
hair into its customary bun. The effort to make herself pre-
sentable had been worth it when she'd emerged from the
hospital to find a crowd of fans cheering at her apparent
recovery. As always, she'd been silently awed and a little
intimidated at being the object of such intense scrutiny. Although she hadn't been willing to admit it at the time, she'd
been grateful for Javier's solid presence beside her. Especially when she'd caught a glimpse of the latest newspaper
headline.

'Don't I have to deal with the police, seeing as Tyson
Blackwell is to be charged?'

'We'll deal with it this afternoon, if you're feeling up to
it. If not, we'll handle it later. I've spoken to the authorities. They don't really need your statement to charge him.'

'They don't?'

He shook his head. 'Angelis had a member of your father's staff watching over you. Blackwell was filmed on video pushing you into making that dangerous jump.' His jaw tightened, his features cast in shadow as the car moved through traffic. 'Why did you do it?'

Her breath emerged shakily as memory slashed across her mind. Her father had finally confessed, after condemning her for wanting to sever their professional relationship, that he'd gambled all her money away. Their only asset—albeit a heavily mortgaged one—was the estate in Tuscany.

'I had a lot on my mind that morning. I wasn't thinking clearly. And before you think me completely foolish, I'd done the jump successfully over a dozen times in the days before.'

'Was your lack of concentration to do with Angelis? Or the chaos your father has made of your finances?'

She gasped. 'You know about that?'

'Your father has been pursuing this deal for the better part of a year, each time asking for more money. You didn't think I'd do my homework on why he was so eager to sign you away?'

Her insides chilled. 'So you know—'

'I know everything, *querida*. And I have you in the proverbial palm of my hand. I can ruin you with the snap of my fingers.'

That debilitating state of ennui that had assailed her on and off over the past few weeks wove over her again. The urge to give up, walk away from it all, *now*, rather than later as she'd tried to discuss with her father, was so strong it caught her breath.

'Did you hear me, Carla?'

'Loud and clear. You can ruin me. You can breathe fire. You can command the very heavens to crush me into a speck of dust. I acknowledge your almighty power over me. But please excuse me if I don't genuflect. I'm battered and bruised enough as it is.'

A dark look entered his eyes. 'What's wrong with you? And I don't mean physically. Your apathy is unbecoming in an athlete of your calibre. You haven't risen to number one by being cowed by a few challenges.'

She laughed, the sound scratching her throat. 'So you not only expect me to jump when you say how high, but I should have an attitude when I do it?'

'I'm saying representing my company with such a defeatist demeanour will not work.'

'I'll work on practising my positive mental attitude before I step in front of the camera. Is that enough for you?'

'This isn't a joke, Carla.'

'Trust me, I'm well aware of that.

She felt his probing stare for several minutes. But thankfully, he didn't press her further before they drew up to the five-star hotel in the heart of Rome.

The hotel was renowned for its ultra-private accessibility to celebrities and she breathed a sigh of relief when they were ushered through a discreet entrance and into the private lift that serviced the penthouse.

Carla walked into the sumptuously decorated room and halted when she saw her father. Beside him, several familiar-looking suitcases were stacked neatly on a caddy, which a butler was in the process of wheeling away.

The ragged notion that she was once again being managed, herded where Olivio Nardozzi wanted her to be, tore through her.

'I have a few phone calls to make,' Javier announced once he'd acknowledged her father's greeting. 'I'll leave you two to catch up. Carla, dinner will be served at eight. Make sure you rest before then.'

Before she could respond, he strode off down the hallway. She told herself his abrupt absence didn't affect her as much as the mild hollowing of her stomach indicated.

She stiffened as her father placed the crystal tumbler

he'd been drinking from on a nearby antique cabinet and crossed the room.

'*Mia figlia*, it's good to see you on your feet again. I wanted to be there when you were released, but I was assured that everything was in hand. How are you feeling?'

She didn't react as he leaned forward and kissed her cheeks. When he stepped back, she glimpsed the tight, haggard look on his face.

'I'm fine,' she replied, desperately squashing any heartache she felt over the state of their relationship. Her father had long driven home to her that he abhorred any show of emotion, especially that of weakness. In all things she was expected to be poised, controlled. Emotionless. It was the reason their ongoing rows writhed like a live wire between them.

'I hope your time in hospital has brought you to your senses?' he murmured in Italian.

Anguish ripped through her. 'If by my senses you mean I've given up my bid to lead an independent life, then I'm sorry to disappoint you but my wishes remain the same,' she whispered fiercely. 'I'm still taking a break from ice skating, and no, I haven't made up my mind how long that break will be. When I decide, I'll let you know.'

'Does Santino know about this ludicrous decision of yours? I don't believe that he does, or your contract would be in serious jeopardy by now and we'd be on our way to court.'

She bit her lip. Her contract with Javier's company didn't specifically state that she couldn't make the decision she intended to take, but she doubted he would be pleased to learn she might lose her number-one-ranking status before she'd fulfilled the full terms of her sponsorship deal.

'Contracts can be renegotiated. Nothing is set in stone yet. I'll tell him when I'm ready. And I'd thank you to stay out of that decision.'

Her father's espresso-coloured eyes hardened. 'You forget yourself, girl. You wouldn't be where you are today without me.'

'Without your punishing strive for perfection and the strict rules that ensured I had no life outside figure skating, you mean?' she sniped, the ennui rushing away to be replaced by the haunting reality of what she'd let her life become. And she couldn't even fully blame her father for that.

'I moulded you and ensured your iconic place in the history books!'

'Through fear and intimidation. At each turn you threatened to abandon me just like—' She pulled herself up short, sucking in a deep breath.

'Go on, say it. Just like your *mamma* left you?'

Her hurt escalated until her whole body was engulfed in pain. 'And we both know why she left, don't we?'

He slashed an angry hand through the air. 'I refuse to indulge you in this childish need to revisit the past. Your *mamma* is gone, and you dishonour her memory with this petty squabble you insist upon.'

'How dare you accuse me of dishonouring her memory? When you didn't even tell me she was dead until the *morning* of her funeral?'

Olivio's frame tensed, his five-foot-nine stature rigid with banked fury. 'You had a competition to win. I didn't think the news would do anything but throw you off your game.'

Her blood turned cold. 'Every time I think there's a shred of humanity in you, Papà, you prove me wrong.'

His face tightened into a hard, implacable mask. 'I don't know what has got into you these past few weeks. Whatever it is, I suggest you take the time in New York to reassess your priorities. This deal with Santino will be the making of us, if you don't mess it up. In the beginning, I was against him staggering the payments on the basis of your performance, but now I see it's a good thing. It might not be enough to save us from the bank's red letters, but if it helps keep you in line—'

'You forget I'm no longer a child. Your threats of abandonment don't frighten me any more!'

'And I haven't come this far for you to suddenly develop whimsical delusions. Only has-beens and losers scurry away with the excuse to *find* themselves. You're number one and you'll remain number one—'

'Or you'll what? Drive me to another convent like you did when I was ten years old and threaten to leave me there unless I behaved? I'm not ten any more.'

'No, you're not. But you signed a contract to keep me as your manager until you're twenty-five, and I won't be got rid of that easily. I'll take you to court if I have to.'

A vice squeezed in her chest. 'You'd do that? To your own daughter?'

'The daughter you were six weeks ago wouldn't have made these ridiculous demands. I'm not sure what happened after the charity gala—'

'Don't plead innocence, Papà. I found out that you'd tried to bribe Draco's fiancée into leaving him so you could marry me off to him! Do you know how it made me feel to hear that from Maria?' she rasped.

'I was only acting in your best interests. You were infatuated with him once. It seemed the sensible option to secure your future with his.'

She curled her fingers into fists, and winced when her broken wrist protested. 'This isn't the Middle Ages! My future is mine and mine alone to secure as I please.'

His lips pursed. 'That's where you're wrong. If you think I'm going to stand by and—'

'I think it's time for you to leave your daughter to rest, Olivio,' Javier intoned from the entrance to the hallway.

Carla started. It was a testament to his predatory stealth that neither she nor her father had heard him return to the living room. Studying his face, she tried to gauge how much he'd overheard. A flick of his gaze to hers told her he'd heard and understood enough.

And had once again acted as judge, jury and executioner.

Fed up to the back teeth of being embroiled in manipulative parents and male egos, she glared at him. 'Please stay out of this.'

Javier ignored her, his laser gaze on her father. 'I'll let you be the judge of whether you think this is the right time to be airing your…questionable family laundry.'

The statement was aimed at the heart of Olivio's pride. And he responded predictably. '*Sì*, you're right. This isn't the time or place. I will join you in New York, *cara*, when you're better recovered.'

The pecks on her cheeks were cold and emotionless, and she wondered why he'd even bothered. Yes, of course. Appearances.

She stood frozen as he shook hands with Javier, and left.

Slowly, Javier sauntered to where she stood.

'Do you intend to stand there all day?' he mocked.

'I intend to do my very best to avoid being in the same room with you as much as possible,' she snapped.

His nostrils flared. 'Watch it, Principessa. There are only so many insults I'm prepared to take until something gives.'

Carla forced herself to exhale calmly. 'You feel the same way, Javier. Don't pretend otherwise.'

'Don't presume to know what I'm feeling.'

'Fine. Whatever. Please tell me where my suitcases have been taken. I'd like to get changed.'

He regarded her for several tense seconds, then turned away. She followed him down the hallway till they reached two sets of double doors. Javier swung open the right set and walked into the room.

As with every inch of the penthouse, the suite was decorated from top to bottom with classic luxury that drew the eye to the blend of contemporary and antique pieces around the room. The ceiling had retained its lofty rococo design and rich parted drapes offered early evening views of Rome and the Vatican in the far distance.

But it was the bed that drew her eye. It was queen-sized and mounted on a double dais; the silk coverlet alone made her want to lie down and let its decadent luxury relax all her troubles away. Or was it something else entirely that drew her attention to that particular piece of furniture?

Heat rushed through her as she remembered another time. Another bed. An uninhibited period in time that had haunted her ever since.

'If you need anything, there's an intercom next to the bed that summons the butler.'

His tone was gravel rough enough to pry her attention from her dangerous memories. Her eyes met his, and, far from the cool regard of moments ago, his gaze contained a banked fire that stopped her breath.

'Okay...thank you.'

He jerked out a nod. Expecting him to leave, she waited. And felt a renewed surge of heat when his eyes conducted a slow, thorough appraisal of her. She wanted to tell him to stop, to truly leave her be. But the words stuck in her throat as the sinful attraction she couldn't seem to suppress around him engulfed her once more.

A rough sound ripped through the room. It could've come from her.

They moved at the same time—she sideways, striking for the bed. Javier lunged in her direction, then veered sharply towards the door.

'Wait.'

He froze. Turned.

'I... I wish I didn't have to ask, but...'

He frowned. 'Spit it out, Carla.'

'My zipper.' She held up her immobilised wrist. 'I won't be able to reach it with this. Could you help me, please?'

He executed a smooth return to where she stood. 'Are you sure you want my help? After all, it would involve me touching you. And I know how you feel about that,' he jeered.

She lifted her chin. 'Fine. I'll get your butler to help me.'

Before the words were fully out, her waist was grasped in a firm hold. 'Take one more step towards that door and I'll make you regret it,' he growled.

With a mere foot separating them, his warm breath washed over her face as he exhaled.

'Seriously, stop tossing out threats like confetti. It's getting old.'

One corner of his mouth quirked as he placed a finger beneath her chin and lifted her gaze to his. 'You've got a little spark back. My investment may not be in danger, after all. Turn around,' he rasped.

She held his gaze a second longer, suddenly unsure if this was such a good idea. Surely, staying in her clothes around him was better than what she was about to subject herself to? But changing her mind now was out of the question.

Swallowing, she presented her back to him. The air thickened, wrapping them up in a sultry heat as the seconds ticked by. His breath tickled her exposed nape, her body responding to that ephemeral contact by firing up her nerve endings.

His knuckles brushed her spine and Carla squeezed her eyes shut. The rasp of the zipper was amplified in the heavy silence, every inch of exposure making her heart race faster. The silk and lace teddy she wore beneath provided shockingly inadequate cover, her skin on fire from Javier's gaze.

An eternity later, his hands dropped. 'It is done.' His voice was rough, barely civil.

He was gone before she'd exhaled the air trapped in her lungs. She stumbled to the bed and sank down, her chest rising and falling with an urgency that had nothing to do with her diminished health.

Limbs trembling, she kicked off her shoes, released her hair from its knot, tugged back the covers and slid into bed, grateful for the momentary peace to gather her thoughts.

All her life she'd been caught between a rock and a hard place—please her father or bear his wrath, achieve excellence at all costs or have a life. The feeling that she was once again caught in a pincer-like situation drew a ragged sob from her throat.

Mildly shocked at the tears once again filling her eyes, she dashed them away, but they fell faster, thicker. She firmed her lips. No way was she crying over her lot in life. She would heal. She would find a way out of the situation with her father. Most of all, she would discover once and for all what had happened to her mother.

Because she didn't think she could live with the thickening shadow that she'd had anything to do with it.

CHAPTER FOUR

CARLA SURFACED FROM sleep to the sound of knocking. Momentarily disoriented, she tried to sit up, and winced as horrendous pain shot up her arm. Belatedly recalling her broken wrist, she adjusted herself and cradled her sore limb.

Another round of hard knocking shook the doors of the suite, before they swung open. Javier stood in the doorway, minus his jacket. With his sleeves rolled up, his arms were exposed in all their bronze, muscled glory.

She pried her gaze away from his arms and looked up as he approached. 'By all means, come in,' she muttered.

His features locked in a frown. 'I've been knocking for several minutes. You didn't answer.'

She hadn't planned on sleeping, had lain in bed for almost an hour, lost in her thoughts before sleep had finally claimed her. She slid her hands through her hair, noting that, although her dreams had been troubled, she felt even stronger than before.

About to respond, she jerked back as Javier took her chin in a firm hold.

'You've been crying. Why?'

She gave a bitter laugh. 'Why do you care?'

'Answer me.'

She shrugged. 'I have no idea.'

His grip tightened just a touch. 'Try again.'

'It's true. I'm not a crier. Probably not since I was ten years old. But I guess there's a second time for everything.'

'I doubt that I have the power to reduce you to tears, so this has something to do with your father and your ongoing partnership, *si*?'

She glared at him. 'Will you let it be if I say it's none of your business?'

An unfathomable emotion hardened in his eyes. 'Not if you've been lying here feeling sorry for yourself because of it.'

She wrenched herself from his grasp, partly annoyed with herself because that was exactly how she'd been feeling. She'd also realised that for the first time in her life she didn't have a punishing schedule to take her mind off the bleakness of her life. Hiding the abject hollowness the thought brought, she pushed a swathe of hair off her face. 'Did you want something in particular, or did you interrupt my me time just for the hell of it?'

His sumptuous mouth tightened before he strolled to the dressing room. Returning with a silk robe-like gown in rich, vibrant colours, he held it out to her. 'Dinner will be served in twenty minutes. You don't need to get dressed if you intend to return here straight afterwards for more of your *me time*.'

Shock gaped her mouth as she took the robe from him.

'You look surprised. You forget that I want you healthy as quickly as possible. There's only so long I can put launches on hold before schedules become impossible to handle.'

She gave a false smile. 'And here I thought you were doing this out of the goodness of your heart.'

He returned her smile with an equally false one. 'You'll soon learn that goodness and heart aren't terms most people apply to me, *querida*. But I do draw the line at decimating the sick and weak.' He jerked his chin at the robe. 'Do you need help putting that on?'

She noticed she was crushing the soft material in her fist and quickly smoothed it out. 'No. Thanks.'

He left as abruptly as he'd entered, leaving the space he'd occupied significantly less vibrant than it'd been before. Realising she was staring into thin air, she shook out the robe. The kimono-style arms offered no restriction for her bound wrist and she wondered if that was why Javier had chosen it. Then she caught sight of the discreet hotel label and realised she was affording him more courtesy than he was worth.

The scent of rich pasta and aromatic sauces hit her nostrils the moment she entered the hallway. Her stomach growled, whether to remind her that she hadn't eaten a proper meal for days or that the meal she was heading for would fall outside her regime, she didn't know. But she followed her nose to the dining room to find Javier approaching from the terrace.

He cradled a glass of red wine from which he sipped slowly without taking his eyes off her. She watched him savour the drink for several moments before he swallowed. 'You've lost weight.'

She dragged her gaze from the thick masculine column of his throat. 'Being in hospital for a few days will do that to you.'

He walked to where she'd stopped at the place setting on the dining table. 'You were already too thin when I saw you in New York a month ago,' he countered. 'Now you look even worse.'

Stung by his words, she focused on the silverware. 'What a delightful start to our dinner, you hurling insults at me.'

'I'm not hurling insults, merely stating a fact.'

'In case you need me to spell it out to you, I need to maintain a certain weight for my career.'

She was unprepared for the slide of his hand at her temple, the soft caress of her jaw before he tucked a strand of hair behind her ear. Her breath locked in her throat as he murmured, 'You forget, *cara*, that I'm intimately familiar with your body. I've availed myself of every inch of it. It may have been three years, but I remember each curve and hollow vividly. Now you have fewer curves and more hollows. I don't like it.'

Carla shivered at the low, sizzling delivery. 'Javier—'

'Whatever it is you're pining for, it's time to put it out of your mind,' he sliced at her as if she hadn't tried to respond.

'Nothing and *no one* is worth what you're putting yourself through,' he finished, his eyes narrowed and laser-focused.

She bristled. 'You think I can get over whatever it is I'm feeling just by snapping my fingers?' she demanded, incredulous.

'I believe the only person standing in your way of achieving your goals is you. Your destiny is yours to mould or throw away by the choices you make. Or by dwelling on what you can't have.' He pulled out her chair and motioned her into it.

Carla sat down, fascinated against her will and more than a little bewildered by the words falling from his mouth. 'And how has that wisdom served you?'

He spread his arms and displayed himself with shameless arrogance. 'According to the world's most successful magazine, I'm the perfect embodiment of personal and professional success. I encapsulate the very essence of work/life balance. I'm therefore the envy of every red-blooded male on the planet. Who am I to argue with that pronouncement?' he asked drolly.

'I see that you're not letting the accolade go to your head or anything.'

His lips twitched as he reached over to pour her a glass of water. But the gaze he sent her was anything but amused. 'I demand perfection. You're currently several degrees below par. You know this as well as I do. It's time to change that. You can start by eating a decent meal.'

Before she could blink, her plate was heaped with pasta and a thick, creamy sauce. Freshly baked focaccia bread spread with garlic butter was presented on a platter, along with Parmesan cheese, which Javier held out with a pointed look.

He was testing her.

Her stomach growled.

With a purse of her lips, she gave in.

The first taste had her groaning. She would hate herself

in the morning. Or congratulate herself for taking the first step in claiming her life back. Whatever. She was determined to enjoy this meal in its entirety. Which was just as well because she had no recollection of finishing her portion, only of Javier heaping another serving onto her plate and presenting her with the bread again.

She took it slower the second time, her gaze drawn repeatedly to his elegant hands as he swirled his wine.

'I'm not used to having free time on my hands. I'll go crazy sitting in one place for two weeks,' she said, striving for something to dwell on beside his hands.

'I figured as much. When we get to New York, depending on your recuperation progress, you can start familiarising yourself with the products you'll be working with.'

She frowned. 'Am I allowed to know what they are now? The contract didn't specify.'

'For confidentiality reasons.' He shrugged. 'I see no harm in telling you now. The first one will be the new line of JS1 speedboats. They're set to launch in two months' time, right before the summer.'

She broke a piece of bread and soaked up the sauce on her plate. 'I know nothing about speedboats.' But she could learn, especially if she had the time off from ice skating that she was planning. She glanced at him, debating whether this was the right time to tell him of her future plan.

'It's a good thing I have total belief in your superb acting skills, then,' he replied.

The atmosphere changed, the air clogging with silent, deadly waves of recrimination. It effectively killed any attempt to inform him of her decision, the bite of bread turning sour so she struggled just to chew and swallow it.

'We won't be able to work well together if you insist on bringing up the past every time I say something you don't like,' she pointed out.

'And that bothers you?'

She glanced up from her plate, bemused that he would

ask so obvious a question. 'Of course it does. We had a one-night stand that ended badly. I admit I was at fault—'

'How magnanimous of you,' he drawled with an edge that set her nerves jangling.

'I didn't really know what I was doing, okay?' she blurted, exasperation and shame duelling within her. 'I was younger and less wise than I am now. I was also rebelling against...' She stopped and took a breath.

'Against?' he pressed.

'I wanted to be a normal twenty-one-year-old. I wanted to experience *life*. My every experience before that night... before Miami had been punishingly regimented. The pressure was just piling on, and I wanted a little...reprieve.'

'So you used me, then made sure I knew I'd been used and discarded?' he condemned icily.

'My reaction the next morning wasn't great. I know that.' She cringed in remembrance. 'But I didn't deliberately set out to sleep with you.'

His features froze in a granite mask. 'Are you saying I somehow forced you into bed with me?'

'No, of course not! But being with you was...an extremely intense experience, Javier. I was completely out of my depth,' she confessed.

Silence descended on the table. It was a good thing she was full because Carla didn't think she could take another bite without choking. Javier's expression remained shuttered, his gaze downcast as he stared into his wine glass.

'I came on strong because you gave me every indication that you wanted me just as badly as I wanted you. I don't mind admitting that the greedy hunger in your eyes when you looked at me coupled with the ingénue air about you turned me on.' He gave a low, self-deprecating laugh. 'You had me so fooled, I nearly punched my own friend's lights out, remember? Little did I know that I was playing directly into your hands.'

The shame that had been crawling along her skin thickened. She tried to block out the memory, but it raged full and large and unavoidable.

Newly turned twenty-one, she'd negotiated a two-week break after winning another world championship and managed to wangle an invitation to spend the time off in New York with her best friend Maria and Draco. Revelling in nothing but new delights like shopping, attending her first nightclub and even sneaking in her first taste of champagne, she'd never wanted the vacation to end. She especially hadn't wanted to return to Tuscany to a father who had turned increasingly demanding and unreasonable in the weeks leading up to her twenty-first birthday. In a desperate bid to find common ground, and simply because they hadn't spoken in several months, Carla had called her mother and pleaded with her to intervene with her father.

Hoping the brief conversation would yield the results she wanted, she'd naïvely thrown herself into her last weekend of freedom by accompanying Draco and Maria to Miami. Little had she known that she'd set in motion a chain reaction of events that would haunt her for the rest of her life. Her father's phone call branding her a disappointment and a traitor had come an hour into the party hosted by Javier Santino.

The strange, tingling feeling she'd experienced when she'd met the enigmatic, devastatingly handsome Spanish man had only been superseded by her father's decimating condemnation. Years-long feelings of oppression had exploded, leading to a desperate and blind search for oblivion. With Maria nowhere to be found, she'd indulged in one too many tequila slammers, until Draco's tough-love dressing-down had sent her fleeing to the bathroom. She'd emerged to find Draco and Javier engaged in a heated argument, and, unwilling to face any more censure from Draco, she'd readily accepted Javier's invitation to go for a walk. Truth be told, she hadn't needed another excuse to be with Javier, his breathtaking looks and clear interest much more than she'd ever been used to.

Draco's displeasure with her decision had been clear, as had Javier's irritation with him. Only after numerous reassurances that she'd be fine had Draco backed down.

She'd let Javier take her hand, his formidable possessiveness a new and exciting danger she'd yearned for. Besides being with a man who made her every breath quiver, being firmly entrenched in the present had meant there was no room to think about her father. Or her mother. Or what her attempt to find her own sense of worth and happiness would mean.

The ride in his open-top sports car to the 'best coffee place in town' had ended with an incandescent, mind-blowing kiss hours later on a secluded pier, and quickly progressed back to the now empty beachfront mansion.

'Are you sure you want this?' he'd asked her several times in between tugging off her shoes, disposing of her handbag, pulling the diamond-studded clip from her hair and showering compliments as he kissed every inch of exposed skin.

A bold hand cupped him, his girth momentarily stopping her breath. 'I want to experience everything you have to give, Javier. Please don't make me wait.'

His groan echoed through her entire being. 'Say things like that to me and I'll have to take you right here on the stairs.'

'Tell me the right words to say. Teach me what pleases you.'

'*Madre di Dios.* Either you've done this enough to know that it's guaranteed to drive any man crazy,' he growled, 'or...'

'Or what?'

Golden brown eyes bore into hers. 'Or you're a sexually potent creature who doesn't even know her own power.'

'I'm...neither. I've never done...this before.'

Shock. Surprise. Blazing possessiveness coupled with something so primitive, every cell leapt with sizzling excitement. Then a bold cupping of her nape. 'Say that again, *mi corazón*. Explain it to me explicitly so there's no mistaking what you're saying to me.'

'I've never slept with anyone, Javier. I'm a virgin.' Shaky words, spoken with dread that her confession would end the most transcendent experience of her life.

'I'm to be your first?' Disbelief and a touch of reverence in his words.

'Y...yes. If you want to be.' She squeezed her eyes shut and reframed the words. 'I want you to be the first. Please don't refuse me.'

'Refuse you? Do you have any idea what the thought of you saying this...or asking another guy to be your first, does to me?'

Breath punched from her lungs, refilling an instant later with cautious hope. 'No...?'

'Let me show you.'

Scorching kisses branded her, leaving her gasping for breath, her fingers clenched in his hair as he swung her into his arms and strode for the nearest flat surface, which happened to be the first-floor hallway wall. Her silver sequinned dress seemed to melt off her body, along with the white bra and thong set, which particularly aroused a torrent of guttural Spanish words. His exploration of her was thorough, his fierce and expert attention eliciting an uninhibited response from her.

'Do you feel this, *querida*? Do you feel how much I want you?'

His erection, thick and heavy between her thighs, brought flames to her cheeks and a fire low in her belly. 'Yes.'

The involuntary twitch of her hips earned her a heart-stopping smile.

'You're a natural sensualist, but I'm going to enjoy teaching you so much more.'

'Yes.'

She was lost in delirium, the sound of the condom opening barely breaching her consciousness. Exploring him as thoroughly as he explored her became a need she couldn't... didn't want to deny. Swift, hesitant kisses grew longer, bolder, her teeth and tongue coming into play when harsh, throaty encouragement fell from his lips. A pinch of his flat nipple brought a deep shudder, making her freeze in alarm.

One strong hand captured both of hers an instant later. 'As much as I love that, you've shoved me to breaking point very quickly, Carla *mia*.' A kiss on her swollen lips, before he dropped to his knees before her. A firm grip on her thigh parted her legs. 'I need to redress the balance a little.'

The brazen possession of her sex with his mouth brought a scream that echoed through the hallway. The descent into lustful madness was instantaneous and comprehensive as pleasure imploded through her. The onslaught of her first orgasm was a stunningly unique experience that suspended time itself.

The sensation of being thrown over one broad shoulder and carried to his vast, palatial bedroom remained a delicious haze, very soon after replaced by the vivid reality of Javier, gorgeous, powerful and intensely aroused, his face stamped with carnal intent as he loomed over her.

Dark eyes locked onto hers. 'I can't wait to make you mine, *tesoro mio*.'

'*Sì*...please.'

'Wrap your legs around my waist. Tighter.'

The broad head of his erection nudged her opening. Nerves pinched at her excitement. The lower lip she bit in agitation was kissed free, his tongue probing her mouth to fan the flames of desire engulfing her.

Sweet languidness stole through her. Javier thrust swift and deep, then grimaced at her sharp scream.

'*Lo siento, querida*. Forgive me, it couldn't be helped.' Sure hands caressed her cheeks and throat, kisses planted on her lips until the hurt subsided.

Decadent fire soon replaced the ache, the residual discomfort trailing away to leave a sensation so unique and incredible, her mouth dropped open in wonder when he pulled back and slowly thrust again.

'Javier,' she breathed.

'*Sí*, I know,' he groaned, a deep shudder moving through him as he repeated the move. 'I wondered whether this chemistry was only in my imagination,' he confessed, the look in his eyes almost bashful. 'You have no idea how much it pleases me that it is not.'

Delight at her part in this indescribable union brought a sultry smile. 'I think I have *some* idea.'

His deep, low laugh, almost as captivating as what was happening to her, stopped her breath. The inkling that something totally out of her control was taking place in this bed, in this room, skittered over her skin.

It evaporated a second later when he moved again. Then she was hanging on for dear life, every emotion she'd ever experienced paling into insignificance in the face of the raw, unadulterated pleasure spinning her into oblivion.

The oblivion continued deep into the night, each experience unbelievably better than the last.

And then morning arrived.

A glance at the man she'd given her innocence to sent her emotions into freefall. She'd read somewhere that you never forgot your first. Javier Santino had attained unforgettable status even before they'd shared their first kiss.

As she lay there, Carla let herself wonder what it would be like if her life were different…if Javier were a permanent fixture and not a painfully temporary one…if the quick Internet search she'd done in the bathroom last night hadn't compared his affairs to high-octane roller-coaster rides—blood-pumping, exhilarating, but over in a blink of an eye.

'*Buenos dias, cariño.*'

Carla would never know whether it was the deep, sexy greeting or the firm tug of demanding hands she never wanted to let her go that had done it.

But the fear that she was already addicted to this…to Javier…had been real and immediate and frightening, and yet another dimension to a complicated life she couldn't afford.

Pushing him away, she leapt out of bed, keeping her back to him so her bewildered feelings wouldn't show. 'I have to go.'

'What's the hurry? It's Sunday. Let me feed you breakfast, then we can spend the day however you want. Personally, I'd prefer we stay in bed, but—'

'No! What happened last night…it's not going to happen again,' she forced out.

Tense silence finally made her glance over her shoulder. She glimpsed the stony, puzzled expression on his face. And fled.

He caught up with her in the hallway where she was busy tugging on her dress. 'What the hell's going on, Carla?'

Several avenues of explanation opened up before her, most of which revolved around newly emerging *feelings*. None of which she could voice.

So she shrugged. 'Draco will be wondering where I am. I need to get back to him.'

Nostrils flared with displeasure. 'Or you could use that incredible invention called the phone and let him know you're with me,' he rebutted.

The temptation to do that lanced her, terrifying her with its brutal insistence. What on earth was wrong with her? 'I'd much rather leave.'

Urgent hands grabbed her. 'Do you regret what we did last night?'

She opened her mouth to deny his words. To tell him that last night had been the most extraordinary night of her life. But he was giving her the perfect out, a way to retreat with her new, terrifying feelings intact.

'Yes, it was a mistake. I wish it hadn't happened.' Because now it had, she knew, bone-deep, that no other man, no other relationship would compare. And he wasn't in it for the long run.

Javier paled. 'What?'

She tried to move, but he held on. 'Javier, let me go.'

'Explain yourself first, Carla. Did I hurt you?' he whispered raggedly.

'No, you didn't.'

'Then why?'

At her stubborn silence, he cupped her chin and drew her face up. She watched myriad emotions transition over his face until a cold gleam slowly lit his eyes. 'You used me to divest yourself of your virginity, is that it?'

'I—what?' she returned, stunned.

'What's the matter? Angelis doesn't like virgins, so you thought you'd use me to take care of your little problem and now you're running back to him?'

Her mouth dropped open, shock rendering her speechless. Then, realising once again that he was handing her the perfect excuse, she raised her chin higher. 'Yes. I want to go back to Draco, if you don't mind.'

She was still reeling from the wrong turn of events when he dragged her down the stairs, flinging her shoes and handbag at her on the way. 'Get the hell out of my sight.' He wrenched the front door open. 'And, Carla?'

He waited until she turned, her insides shaking at the fury in his face.

'*S-sì?*'

'Pray that we never meet again. Because every single nightmare you've ever had will pale in comparison to what I'll do to you.'

'Was it worth it?' a hard, cold voice demanded.

Carla was yanked from the depths of vivid memories. She blinked hard and tightened her muscles when she realised her whole body was shaking with the force of her residual feelings.

'Was what worth it?' she asked obliquely, struggling to bring her mind back to the present.

'Sacrificing yourself in my bed to get Angelis's attention and make him jealous.'

She clenched her jaw. 'I don't know how many times I need to say it before you believe me. Draco had nothing to do with what happened between us. You made assumptions... and I just took advantage of the excuse.'

'And yet you were dating your *excuse* a month later,' he snarled.

'My mother died. He came to the funeral in England. He took me out a few times to try and distract me, that's all. Afterwards, when his sister was hurt, I spent some time with *both* of them, helping her get through it. That was all that happened.'

His lips curled. 'I may have been an outsider with a vivid imagination conjuring scenarios out of thin air. But didn't your own father try to forge a more permanent deal between you and Angelis only a few weeks ago?'

She couldn't hide from the truth. 'That doesn't mean it was what *I* wanted. And why does it upset you so much, anyway?' she threw at him.

Dark brown eyes turned to icy chips. 'No one likes to be used and tossed away like rubbish.'

She bit her lip, knowing whatever she said would come out wrong. But she couldn't stand the tension. 'We need to get past this.'

His eyes turned colder. 'Do we? What about the sound bite you gave the reporter who interviewed you after your championship win three years ago? Correct me if I'm wrong but wasn't it along the lines of, "Javier is a playboy. I don't date playboys"? Oh, and I believe someone from your *camp* followed that a few weeks later with another quote, calling me "an individual with low morals and a questionable pedigree"? Do we need to get past *those* too?'

Ice drenched her soul. From her fingertips to her toes, she lost all feeling in her limbs as she stared at him.

The events of the morning after their one-night stand had been bad enough, but this… Carla swallowed. Now she truly understood Javier's cold fury.

Understood that she appeared to have dealt a far deeper, much more personal injury to his pride.

CHAPTER FIVE

JAVIER WATCHED HER grow paler by the second, her green eyes pools of deep shock as she stared at him.

'What are you talking about? I-I didn't say anything about your pedigree…or the low morals thing,' she stammered.

'But you admit the playboy *thing*?' he drawled.

'I was just…there were rumours about us after your party. I was just trying to—'

'Distance yourself from the man who could ruin your "innocent princess" image?'

He watched her jaw tighten. 'No, I wanted to kill the rumours once and for all. Besides, I didn't think you'd welcome the association with me.'

'So you threw me under the bus to save me? How ingenuous—or should I say *ingenious*—of you.'

She swiped a shaky hand across her forehead. 'I'm sorry! The reporter caught me off-guard. As for the other thing, I know nothing about it. Even if I did, I'd never say anything like that,' she implored.

He'd investigated the source of those rumours, knew it was someone in her management team who'd made that damaging statement when questioned about Javier's association with her. Watching her try to wriggle herself off the hook, he wondered how he could think straight with the fury pounding through his blood.

'It's easy to be remorseful after the event, isn't it? And, *sí*, Principessa, my parentage *is* questionable. I'm the bastard son of an aristocrat. It's a circumstance I accepted long ago. But that didn't give you the right to go digging for it, then airing it in public for your own petty amusement.'

Her mouth worked, no doubt searching for more lies to excuse her behaviour. He waited for it, detachedly interested to see how she extricated herself from this latest stain on her character. He'd meant the words he'd thrown at her when he'd kicked her out of his house in Miami. At the time, a part of him had reeled at how desperately he'd wanted their one-night stand to continue. She should've been forgettable, the decision to create an immediate distance between them the morning after *his* to make.

Instead he'd kept up with any news on her career and personal life. And reeled even further at her heartless slurs on his reputation.

She cleared her throat. 'Javier…please—'

He stopped her meaningless words with a dismissive wave. 'Save it. What puzzles me is how can you be so exceptionally talented in one discipline of your life and yet fail so abysmally in every other aspect?'

She flinched. But slowly her head rose, her eyes meeting his boldly. Hell, she even had the gall to raise one perfect eyebrow at him.

'So…here we are, Javier. What happens next?'

He took his time swallowing the last of his wine, wishing it were something stronger, more bracing with a numbing after-effect. 'Don't worry, *querida*. The lessons I intend to teach you will be delivered in good time.'

Her swift inhalation allayed a little of his fury. She would never know how damaging the revelation about his parentage had been. It'd handed his father the perfect excuse to deny him the only thing he'd ever asked of him. The one thing he'd promised his mother on her deathbed—a proper burial with the family who'd rejected her because of her affair with his father, who had been a married man.

Bitterness stained the fury, charging through him with renewed vigour.

Unable to sit still, he surged to his feet. Her head snapped up to meet his gaze, an imploration he had no intention of succumbing to gleaming from the green depths.

When she struggled to her feet and faced him head-on,

he almost felt sorry for her. 'I didn't say those things about your parentage, Javier.'

'But the anonymous tip came from *your* management. Therefore the responsibility and the fault is yours. I have every intention of making sure you own up to it.'

She stumbled back a step. He was reaching out for her protectively with his free hand before he'd fully grasped his own instinctive action. Clenching his traitorous fist, he slammed his glass down, and shoved both hands in his pockets.

Her frailty was an illusion. She didn't need or want his help. She had a backbone of steel when it came to going after what she wanted.

'It's obvious something else is going on here other than you're letting on. Tell me the consequences so I can try and make it right,' she pleaded.

He froze. Part of him reeled that she would finally acknowledge her actions so openly. But then he remembered it was part of her usual machinations, her ability to disarm him with her words.

'It's too late to right the wrongs. All that's left to do is make the reparations.'

'And let me guess, I'll find out what those *reparations* are when you're ready?'

He smiled a mirthless smile. 'See, *chiquita*, you're already learning.'

And because he couldn't stand to watch her treacherous, offensively delectable mouth tremble for another second, he walked out of the living room, out of the suite, and out into the brisk Rome night.

Carla didn't see Javier again until the limo ferrying her to the airport next morning came to a stop next to a stunning private jet. She'd flown in her share of chartered planes—a perk her father had deemed necessary for her image—but the Santino jet screamed a different class, even from the outside.

Tequila-gold, with thin platinum lines running from nose to fin, the aircraft was as visually masterful as its owner, who currently stood framed in the doorway at the top of the short flight of steps, arms folded and his bespoke-suited body projecting an aura of banked impatience.

She alighted, conscious of the brooding gaze on her, and smiled at the doctor who'd turned up at the hotel suite this morning with instructions to check her over. He'd pronounced her fit to travel, then accompanied her to the airport, his reassurance that her further health needs had been taken care of by Signor Santino, in the form of private medical personnel on board the plane, barely registering with Carla.

After Javier had walked out last night, she'd staggered back to her suite in a state of shock. It didn't take a genius to work out who had made those disparaging comments to the press about Javier's parentage.

Her father had been livid when the rumours of her association with Javier had surfaced in the months after her mother's death. Steeped in grief, she'd barely paid attention to the tabloids, had stuck to saying *no comment* after the initial disastrous interview with the journalist the day of her championship win.

She'd made sure after that never to be drawn on a personal subject, not knowing the damage that was being done behind her back. That Javier had been dealt a much heavier blow than to be called a playboy.

She looked up at him now as she mounted the steps, and her stomach fell. Every accusation he'd hurled at her last night was still etched on his face. The light of day hadn't brought an iota of mercy.

Whatever her father's actions had wrought had to be monumental—

'If you dawdle any longer, we'll miss our take-off slot,' he ground out.

She hoisted her handbag onto her shoulder with her unhurt hand and mounted the last step. It brought her within touching distance of his sleek, silently seething perfection. She brought up her immobilised hand and tried to squeeze past him when he made no attempt to move out of her way.

He stopped her with a hand on her waist, his gaze burning into her. 'You're favouring your wrist. Did you aggravate it?'

'No. But I slept badly last night. I'm certain that didn't help,' she murmured.

He looked from her face to her wrist as if examining the cast would determine the truth of her statement. 'Did the doctor give you anything for it?' he snapped.

'I didn't ask.' Her mind had been on something else. Him.

Exasperation piled onto the myriad volatile emotions swirling over his face. Firming his hold, he guided her inside the aircraft, bypassing grouped armchairs and a conference setting to a sitting area complete with a plush double sofa and recliner. Relieving her of her handbag, he placed it on a nearby table and motioned her onto the recliner. He murmured in Spanish to a middle-aged woman in a neat skirt suit before turning back to her. He leaned forward to secure her seat belt and Carla's breath fractured.

He straightened as the woman approached. 'This is Selma. She's part of my company's medical team. She'll give you something for the pain.'

He waited until she'd taken the painkillers and the plane was moving before he started to walk away.

'Javier?' His revelations last night would continue to haunt her unless she did something about it. She cleared her throat when he paused. 'Can we talk, please?'

'There will be enough time for that, if you insist. Right now, I have work to do. And you need to rest.'

She gritted her teeth as he walked away, silently cursing the guilt raking through her. If she'd been as duplicitous and unfeeling as Javier believed she was, she could've shut her eyes and pretended all this didn't affect her. Instead she fidgeted in her seat as the plane took off and they raced east.

Eventually, the medication kicked in. At some point she woke to find a blanket tucked around her and the lights in the sitting area dimmed. A glass of water stood on the table next to her and she drank before once again succumbing to sleep.

She was awoken by Selma, who smiled and informed her that they'd landed and that Javier had already left the plane to head to his office.

Carla told herself the disappointment she felt was because she'd been denied the opportunity to set the record straight. And she kept telling herself that all through the next two weeks of barely seeing Javier. Of Selma, though, she saw a lot, the doctor almost frustratingly efficient in ensuring Carla was fed, watered and medicated within the four walls of Javier's ultra-luxurious Upper East Side penthouse.

Emerging from her assigned bedroom on the morning after being given the all-clear to pursue light work, Carla caught sight of herself in the large gilt mirror gracing the wide hallway, and paused in surprise.

Her skin looked healthy and vibrant and her cheeks had lost the sickly pallor and gaunt hollowness. Her newly shampooed hair, which she'd worn in a tight bun for as long as she could remember, fell in waves around her shoulders, the distinct caramel highlights catching the sunlight.

'Admiring your new and improved self?'

She jumped and turned to find Javier striding towards her. Dressed in an open-necked casual shirt and black jeans, he was the epitome of sophisticated chic, and arresting enough to make her gape for several embarrassing seconds before she regained her focus. 'There was nothing wrong with my old self,' she snapped after recovering from the shock of suddenly seeing him, larger than life and in the flesh.

'That is a subject of much debate,' he returned.

Carla moved away from the mirror. 'What are you doing here?'

Black eyebrows rose. 'At my last recollection, I lived here.'

Heat suffused her face. 'I didn't mean that. I meant, it's Friday. I thought you'd be gone by now.'

'Sorry to disappoint, but if I want to keep my famous work/life balance title I need to take the occasional day off,' he drawled.

'Is that what you're doing? Taking the day off?'

Powerful shoulders hefted a shrug. 'That depends on how well you do with your first assignment.'

She stopped in her tracks. 'Me?'

'Selma tells me you're fit enough to attend a creative meeting or two as long as your wrist is taken care of. She also tells me you're going stir-crazy. Was she wrong?'

'She wasn't,' she hurriedly replied. She looked down at the short tunic she'd thrown on after her shower because it'd been the easiest thing to hand. 'I'll go and change.'

After a swift perusal of her attire, he shook his head. 'You don't need to. The creative director will be here after breakfast. We'll work from here today.'

He headed for the dining room. She followed him into the large, sunlit room. Before now, breakfast had been a solitary affair, eaten with almost absent enjoyment while her mind worried over what Javier had meant by reparation and just how he would exact it from her.

Now as she walked towards the place set for her, she couldn't help recall how the last meal they'd shared had ended.

But looking at him, she could see little trace of the capricious emotion that had leapt from him then. She didn't fool herself into believing it was far from the surface. Javier had bided his time for three years. She didn't doubt that he would be perfectly content to toy with her a while longer yet.

Suddenly reluctant to touch on the subject she'd spent far too many hours dwelling on, she helped herself to a bagel, smothered it with cream cheese, and took a bite. Swallowing it down with a sip of coffee, she risked a glance and found him staring at her over his coffee cup. 'I'm not sure exactly what a creative director does.'

'We'll discuss the preliminary designs I have in mind for you to work with and then decide how best to go about it.'

'Don't I need to be on your speedboat to get the best visuals?'

'The speedboat shoot has been put on hold until you're no longer wearing that cast. My new premium tequila brand launches in six weeks. I've been struggling to find the right person to front it. You'll be the face of it.'

Her hand shook as she set her cup down. 'What?'

'You're not deaf, *querida*.'

'I'd rather not do that, if you don't mind.'

'But I do mind. You drink the stuff, if I remember correctly. In fact you virtually drowned in it at my birthday party three years ago. I fail to see what the problem is.'

'In light of what happened afterwards, do you really think I'm the right candidate to promote your tequila?'

His mouth twisted cruelly. 'Since you insist on convincing me the circumstances of your getting drunk that night no longer exist, it shouldn't be a problem. Besides, you won't be required to drink it, just pretend it's the best thing that's happened to you since the first time you put your ice skates on. That was the single most incredible moment of your life, was it not?'

She drew in a deep, sustaining breath, before she gave in to temptation and slapped his face. 'You obviously mean to torture me at every opportunity. If that's how you get your kicks, then so be it. But if you want our collaboration to have any hope of working, can I suggest we resolve this sooner rather than later?' When one mocking eyebrow started to lift, she ploughed on. 'So I called you a playboy. Where was the lie in that? Were you not a playboy, then? Are you not now? You date as frequently as you change your socks. In fact, I don't think the paparazzi has snapped you with the same woman twice!'

An arrogant smile twitched his lips. 'Have you been keeping tabs on me, *querida*?'

'Hardly. But it's very difficult to avoid seeing a man who flaunts himself as often as you do. If you choose to practise that work/life balance you're so proud of in public, don't complain when people take an interest.'

'Some aspects of my life may be public. You made it your business to dig up private parts about my parentage that were none of your business, and make them public.'

Her breath shuddered out. 'It wasn't me, Javier. It was my father. The only thing I'm culpable of is guilt by association.'

He regarded her for several tense seconds. 'It's not the only thing you're guilty of, *querida*, but we'll leave that for now. As for the tequila shoot, your role in it stands. You're good at *faking* things.' The discreet sound of the concierge's buzzer echoed through the room. Javier rose and rounded the table to where she sat. Bending low, he placed a kiss at her temple. 'You'll excel in this role. I insist on it. Nothing less than perfection will do.'

She still sat frozen in place when he returned a few minutes later with a casually dressed man in tow. Darren O'Hare wore boxy spectacles, behind which his grey eyes twinkled with friendliness.

'Welcome on board. We've had a hell of a time placing the right person for this launch. I was excited when Javier told me we'd landed you. I'm a huge fan,' he said, a faint Irish brogue curling his words.

Careful not to glance at Javier in case the tension between them exploded onto their unsuspecting visitor, she smiled and shook Darren's hand. 'Thank you. I'll do my best to make it work.'

Darren grinned and set down his leather portfolio. 'I've watched a few of your performances online, for research purposes, of course. Outstanding doesn't begin to describe them. Dedication like that translates into everything. You'll knock this shoot out of the park. Then hopefully I can score myself tickets to your next performance. Tickets for the last one sold out within minutes—'

'Perhaps we can get on with discussing what we need Carla to do? That is, of course, if you've finished with your shameless idol-worshipping?'

Darren froze at the bite in his boss's tone. Clearing his throat, he nodded. 'Sure...of course.'

'Great, let's take the meeting in my office.'

He led the way out, his strides swift and purposeful. Grabbing his case, Darren sent her a puzzled glance. Her smile felt as false as her insides felt brittle.

They entered the room to find Javier poised at the head of an oval table, arms folded. In silence, Darren produced poster-sized glossy shots from his case and spread them out on the table.

Carla stared down at the pictures, the attention to detail and the sheer magnificence of the graphics robbing her of breath. It was quite evident that a lot of time and effort had gone into creating the perfect outer package for La Pasión, the signature drink fronted by J Santino Inc.

She read the tag at the bottom of the first graphic.

La Pasión.
Taste The Edge.
Live The Edge.

'That's our slogan for the tequila. My department is working on the script for you and Pavlov.'

'Pavlov Krychek?' she asked, surprised that the Russian ice-skating supremo was on board with the project. His penchant for throwing diva tantrums was well known. He also had the insufferable egotistical delusion that every woman he came across would fall at his feet.

Darren smiled wryly. 'Yes, he was a pain to sign up but—'

'Sadly he'll no longer be part of this campaign,' Javier finished.

Darren blinked in surprise. 'Since when?'

'Since I fired him this morning. He made one demand too many.' His gaze shifted to her, and Carla's breath stalled. 'I don't tolerate divas, male or female. So you'll be on your own for this one. It'll be just you, the bottle and your ice skates.'

Her eyes widened. 'My skates?'

'It's your signature accessory, the essence of who you are. Otherwise you'll be any other dime-a-dozen celebrity with an eye-catching face.'

Darren nodded slowly, clearly still reeling from the shift in proceedings, but catching up quickly. 'I think that could work…'

'It *will* work, much better than the advertising department's initial idea. Perhaps someone should've brainstormed that before resources were wasted trying to land Krychek?'

A bewildered frown creased Darren's brow, as if he had no idea what he was being scolded for. Again his gaze swung to her, and Carla almost felt sorry for him. Javier Santino in this mood meant hell for everyone.

'So when is all this happening?'

Darren's glance slid to her cast. 'The idea was to shoot the ad on a real ice rink. CGI would work, but the real thing would give it much more depth.'

'Once we finalise your costume and script, we'll start with the nightclub shoots. We'll shoot the ice-skating scenes last when you're completely healed,' Javier added. 'In the meantime, Darren will supply you with some in-depth information of the product to read up on.'

'Isn't the script going to suffice?' she asked.

A terse smile curved his lips. 'You train three times a day to be the best at what you do. It's no different for me. I believe in arming myself with as much information as possible in every situation. Since you're part of this project that applies to you too. Knowledge is power. Don't you agree?'

She knew they were talking about something completely different. That he was taunting her—again. 'Yes. Of course.'

'Good.'

'Is there anything else?' he asked his creative director, who'd been watching their interaction with blatant curiosity.

Darren shook his head. 'That's it for now. All the info you need is in the packet including the schedule we hope to achieve. I'm the location scout for the shoot as well so I'll be in touch to arrange a visit to the rink we intend to use. If you have any questions, Carla, my business card is on the first page...' He trailed off when Javier's mouth suddenly flattened. 'Or I'm sure Mr Santino can help you out.'

Carla swallowed, the thought of returning to the ice suddenly chilling her skin.

'Carla?'

She looked up and caught Javier's shrewd glance. 'Yes?'

'What's wrong?'

She glanced away. 'Nothing. I'm fine.'

But she wasn't. The slight trembling that had taken hold when Javier mentioned returning to the ice rink had intensified in the time since. Much as it had every time she'd thought about it since leaving hospital. Unwilling to show her uncontrolled reaction, she turned away from the table.

'That'll be all for now, Darren,' Javier said. 'We'll touch base in the office on Monday.'

'Sure. Uh...great to meet you, Carla.'

She summoned a fuller, warmer smile, then walked to the leather sofa situated to one side of the room. Their low voices registered on the edge of her consciousness as they left the office. She sank into the seat, massaging her temples as she took deep breaths.

Javier hadn't believed nothing was wrong. She wondered why she'd even bothered trying to fob him off. Because he was back seconds later, striding straight over to crouch in front of her.

'Tell me what's going on with you. Now.'

CHAPTER SIX

JAVIER'S TEETH GRITTED as she shook her head. He didn't want to believe it was a refusal to answer him. That would mean he still wasn't getting through to her. That she didn't think he was serious about every last ounce of reparation he intended to extract from her. His gut clenched hard.

'Are you feeling unwell again?'

That would be the only reason he would accept for her behaviour. 'I told you, I'm fine.'

She tried to release herself. He refused to let her go. Holding her still this close would focus her attention on him instead of on other things. Or other men.

His jaw clenched harder, a sliver of self-disgust rising at the way he'd felt when she'd turned her stunning eyes on O'Hare. Bestowed that beautiful but rare smile on him.

Jealous. He'd been consumed with jealousy.

Which was unacceptable.

'Explain to me then why you looked as if you'd fallen into a trance just now.'

She met his gaze for one bold moment, then looked away with a shrug. 'I'm sorry you don't like the way I look when I'm thinking—'

'Don't insult my—*madre de Dios*, look at me when I'm talking to you!'

Her chin angled up. Almond-shaped pools of green glared at him. Instead of raising his annoyance level, it eased a restriction in his chest. 'I'm looking at you. Satisfied?'

'I will be, marginally, when you tell me what's wrong. And for the sake of my sanity, and yours, don't say nothing.'

Her nostrils quivered delicately with the sustaining breath she took. 'Fine. I don't want to return to the ice.'

Javier frowned. 'Not while your wrist is still in a cast,

no. That part of the ad will only be shot once the binding comes off.'

She shook her head, once more inducing a tightening in his gut. 'Can we not just use CGI like Darren suggested?'

'Explain to me why you don't want to use the ice.'

She shifted, her skin sliding against the silk tunic. Memories of how smooth and warm that skin was slashed across his brain, driving heat into his groin. 'Another fall if I'm not careful could set me back even more months. Why risk another injury for the sake of an ad campaign?'

'Because that campaign is paying you millions in sponsorship funds. Funds that could go away very easily if you don't adhere to your part of the agreement. Surely you're not so obtuse as to overlook that?'

'But we have an alternative!'

Javier sensed something else going on. Had the trauma of Blackwell's training left her with something more than just a bodily injury? Would she even tell him if that were the case? Frustrated anger rose to mingle with the irritations pulsing within him. He refused to add hurt to the equation. Because being upset that he was on the outside of something so important to her shouldn't be an issue for him. She was contractually obligated to give him whatever he wanted.

His mind veered to other things that he wanted. Things that had made him stay away from his own penthouse for two weeks because he didn't want to admit to the need hammering beneath his skin.

'The alternative doesn't work for me. So unless you want to tell me the real reason why you're making the request, the original plan stands.'

He waited. And waited some more. Her eyes shadowed, but her defiant chin stayed up, her mouth firming with whatever emotions were surging through her.

'I told you why. Obviously, you disagree. Are we done now? I'd like to get out of here, get some fresh air.'

'Carla—'

'Oh, God, please don't tell me I'm a prisoner too?'

He caught the hand she'd brought up to push him away, the knowledge that she didn't intend to share what was upsetting her hardening into a knot. He set the notion to one side for the moment. 'You're not a prisoner. But you can't go out on your own either. It's not safe.'

She stilled. 'What do you mean?'

'I mean a group of your fans—I believe they call themselves *The Nardozzians*?—are camped downstairs. If you go out on your own, you'll be mobbed.'

She paled. 'I… I didn't know. They weren't here when I went out for a walk yesterday morning.' The hand in his chest balled into a fist, pressed deeper into his flesh, and Javier got the impression she didn't know how clearly her agitation was showing. 'How long have they been here?'

'They arrived last night. Obviously word has leaked that you're in town.'

She closed her eyes for a split second. When she opened them again, her gaze lingered on his jaw. 'Damn, so I can't go out?'

Catching hold of her chin, he tilted her face. Breathed easier when her eyes connected with his. And then, because he couldn't help himself, he brushed his finger down her cheek. 'You can go out, as long as you're accompanied.'

'And who…?' She exhaled. 'You?'

'Me. Especially since I know that one of those fans has been brazen enough to propose to you several times. I believe he's even gone a few steps further and sent you some risqué pictures of himself?'

Her eyes widened. 'How do you know this?'

'When are you going to get it through your head that I know everything that is relevant to know about you?'

A shadow fleeted through her eyes. 'At least you're not purporting to know absolutely everything.'

'Sadly, *carina*, if we knew everything about each other, we wouldn't be here now, would we?'

The shadows deepened. When she tried to turn her head away, he held her still.

'Has he done anything beyond the pictures and the placards?'

Distaste showed on her face. 'He sent a few horrible letters when he was banned from going on my fan webpage.'

The surge of protectiveness took him by surprise. 'I'll make sure he gets the message about keeping clear boundaries.'

Her soft breath feathered over his hand. Despite his every instinct warning him against it, he drew her closer, the mingled scent of her perfume and shampoo washing over his senses.

'He makes me uncomfortable but I think he's harmless.'

'If he makes you uncomfortable then he's already overstepped his mark.'

Her eyes met his, surprise mingling with another emotion he couldn't read. 'Careful, Javier, or I'll confuse you with someone who actually cares one iota about me.'

His fingers slipped around her nape and tightened in her hair. The action lifted her head up further, exposing the flawless, sleek line of her neck. His senses pounded with the need to taste. He barely managed to restrain himself. 'Your confusion would be unfortunate. I'm merely protecting my investment.'

He ignored the hurt that blinked through her eyes. He couldn't lose sight of the repercussions of her and her father's previous actions. Because of them, his beloved mother's last resting place was among strangers, and each day Javier was unable to right that particular wrong was a day too long.

Sliding his fingers from her hair, he stood and shoved his fist in his pocket. 'You want to go out, be ready in half an hour. I have a video conference later.'

'I thought you were taking the day off?' she replied.

'Sadly I'm addicted to the urge to hammer down the next seemingly impossible deal.'

'You mean, the temptation to torture another human being until they buckle under your will?'

His smile felt as if it could crack ice. 'Same difference. So unless you want to be the recipient of my torture tactics, you'll do as I say.'

She muttered under her breath in Italian, the very unladylike statement bringing a reluctant smile to his lips as she hurried out of the room.

A second later, he frowned, dragging his mind from the sylph-like form of the woman whose presence in his life was anything but a laughing matter, to the reason he'd taken a rare day off.

Any trace of mirth evaporated as he contemplated the reason for his videoconference. As usual, his father hadn't given him advance warning nor any assurance that the call Javier had requested would actually take place. The banked rage that resided just beneath his skin every time he thought of the man whose blood ran through his veins threatened to resurge. The knowledge that it was because of Carla that he continued to have to deal with Fernando made him curse inwardly as he paced to the window.

Looking out to the street below, he caught sight of the clutch of Carla's fans across the street, and another form of rage took hold. She might have downplayed the seriousness of her fan's actions, but Javier knew the side-effects of hero worship and the unfortunate decisions that could unfold because of it.

He was a product of such a misstep.

Had his own mother not been blinded by stars in her eyes, she wouldn't have been taken advantage of by an unscrupulous man who saw no harm in ruining an innocent. She wouldn't have wasted her life pining for and chasing a dream that had been unattainable from the start.

Juliana Santino had died long before her time. The official cause had been cancer, but Javier knew sadness and bitter disappointment had played a huge part in his mother's demise. And the man responsible for those debilitating emotions still had a form of power over Javier because of a woman who commanded more power than was permitted over him.

He needed to end it once and for all.

'I'm ready.'

He whirled, disturbed that he'd been so lost in contemplation he'd been unaware of her return. His gaze raked over her and his senses leaped.

Her white skinny jeans moulded her hips and thighs, heeled boots and a white oversized top that insisted on falling off one shoulder drawing attention to her body. With her newly regained weight and better health had come a vibrancy to her skin.

Something hot and urgent jerked within him.

She looked a perfect picture of innocence, but it was deceptive innocence, he reminded himself.

He forced his gaze up from her endless legs. 'Why are you wearing your hair up?' he demanded before he could think the question through.

She held up her cast-encased hand and wriggled her half concealed fingers with a hint of triumph. 'I can move my fingers without it hurting too much now. The brushing took longer than I wanted and the knot isn't the tidiest, but I'm sure it'll stay up.'

He didn't want it to. He wanted her hair flowing over her shoulders, catching the light and making him guess what colour it really was, not scraped up into a careless bun, making her eyes seem huger and her flawless bone structure fracturing his ability to think coherently.

Dios, he was losing it. He growled under his breath.

Casting a searching glance on his desk, he caught up his car keys. 'Let's go.'

She grimaced at the keys. 'We're driving? I thought we were going for a walk?'

'You thought wrong.'

Her eyes sparked green fire. 'I'd much rather walk—'

'Your mob has increased threefold in the last hour. There's no way I'm subjecting you to that. So it's the car or the penthouse. Your choice.'

He knew his tone didn't indicate it was much of one, but he didn't care.

'Can we walk? Once we're away from here, I mean?' she asked.

He clenched his fist around the metal keys, knowing that if he gritted his teeth any harder his jaw would snap, and headed for the door. 'I'll think about it.'

Her mouth pursed, but she didn't protest further. They rode the lift in silence. As they passed the front desk, she greeted the concierge by name and smiled at the hapless fool, who melted into a puddle of adoration. Javier turned away from the nauseating scene, his mood darkening further when he glanced out into the morning sunshine.

She sighed as he handed his keys to the valet to have his car brought up. 'I'd rather brave it outside on my own if you're going to be this grouchy.'

He despised the bolt of alarm that went through him. 'You'd rather contend with that than be with me?' He jerked his thumb at the mob.

She tilted her head to see past him. He watched her eyes widen. The placards had grown bolder since yesterday. One in particular, from her avid fan, made Javier's skin crawl.

'"*Essere il mio, anima e corpo,*"' she muttered the words in her mother tongue. 'Wow, it seems like everyone wants something from me. It doesn't matter that I don't wish to give it. Or that I want something else for myself.'

'It that a dig at me?'

A small, sad smile curved her lips and he couldn't look away from her expression. 'It's an inescapable truth,' she murmured.

'Don't worry, *querida*, I've no intention of letting you be

owned by anyone else, either *in body or in soul*,' he para-
phrased the words on the placard.

He expected a quick comeback or at least a demand for
him to keep his possessive threats to himself. But a glance
showed the shadows were back again. The eyes that met his
were subdued, her mouth pinched.

'Por el amor de Dios,' he grated. 'If you need fresh air
that badly, come on.'

Sliding his hand around her waist, he guided her through
the double doors leading to the underground garage. The
valet accepted the tip eagerly, but his gaze stayed on Carla,
another victim of her charms.

He hurried her into the sports car, marginally appeased
when she came to life, pulling her seat belt across her body
to secure it. He shut her door and was rounding the hood
when his phone pinged.

Activating the app, Javier read the message once, then
again. The piercing disappointment that lanced him was
unwelcome evidence that he'd allowed himself to hope his
father would talk to him this time. Controlling the need to
smash his fist through the nearest wall, he yanked open his
door and slid behind the wheel, acknowledging that perhaps the drive had come at an opportune time. He revved
the engine mercilessly and earned a furtive glance from
his passenger.

'Can I ask if something's wrong without getting my head
bitten off?'

'Besides the unexpected and unwanted gift of having my
afternoon freer than I wished it to be, no, I don't wish to
discuss what's wrong.' He aimed the car at the exit. For his
own peace of mind, he didn't glance at the screaming fans
who surged for the car as soon as they spotted their idol.
Luckily the mid-morning traffic was clear and he breathed
a sigh of relief when the lights turned green. As he put miles
between them and his apartment, she relaxed.

'Was the video conference important?' she asked after a few minutes.

His laugh was abrasive. 'Since it's one I've been waiting five long years to have, you could say that.' He changed lanes, the abrupt move jerking her body against his. Her shoulder bumped his and her scent filled his nostrils. Hunger he didn't want or completely understand tore through him. His grip tightened on the wheel.

'Can't you reschedule it?'

As a touchy subject, it was singularly effective in dousing a little bit of his hunger. 'When it comes to my father, I find myself in the unique position of being on the back foot.'

He cursed himself the moment the words spilled out.

'Your father?' she echoed, wariness flaring in her eyes. 'He's the one you were supposed to conference with?'

'Until he cancelled on me for the fourth time this month.'

He sped through an amber light and onto Madison Avenue.

'Speaking from personal experience, you don't strike me as the type to sit back and let events unfold the way they want to. I'm assuming you know where your father is?' she asked.

Exhaling, he nodded. 'Yes, I do. But before you make the obvious suggestion, perhaps you should know that the last time my father and I were in the same room, we nearly came to blows.'

She gasped. 'What?'

'*Sí, querida.* He's the only person, besides you, who arouses distinctly *primitive* feelings in me.'

Her lips parted, a look of bewilderment crossing her face before she looked out of her window. 'I won't take that as a compliment.'

'My blood rarely gets this fired up so perhaps you should.'

'Not if it incites violent feelings within you.'

'Fired up doesn't necessarily mean violent. I can think of a few ways to express my more nascent emotions.'

Colour flared into her cheeks. 'I don't see how express-ing yourself that way helps with anything.'

'Spare me the false naiveté, Carla.'

She shook her head, and the careless knot of her hair wob-bled. He resisted the urge to hasten its demise and parked on a leafy street.

'I only meant that the problems wouldn't disappear sim-ply because you…indulged yourself in another way.'

'But if I can regress to my baser instincts and make love not war, wouldn't that put me in a better frame of mind?'

'You don't truly believe that, or I wouldn't be here.'

A rare chuckle ripped free. 'Touché.' He flung his door open and went round to help her out. Turning from him, she gazed up at the three-storey brownstone, one of many on the street.

'Where are we?'

He shrugged. 'Somewhere you're guaranteed privacy. Come on.' He walked round the side to a high, wrought-iron gate and entered the security code. The lock sprang open, and he led her through an ivy-laced trellised arch.

For a split second, Javier asked himself why he'd brought her here. There were many quiet parks he could've taken her to. Hell, with his afternoon suddenly free, he could've driven her to Connecticut or the Hamptons for her precious walk.

Her loud, pleased gasp pulled him from his short rumi-nation.

'Wow, this place is stunning!'

He turned and watched her reaction to the place his mother had loved, albeit never wholeheartedly, her deep attachment to her homeland overshadowing any other place on earth.

The smile Carla had so far only bestowed on others shone his way before she rushed past him to the large fountain and waterfall that trickled into an oval pond that still held fat koi. Miniature bonsai trees that his mother had loved to prune were dotted in pots around the garden and almost every type of rose bush budded, ready for the springtime bloom.

Still puzzling why he'd brought her here, he crossed his arms. 'What's the big deal about fresh air, anyway? Air is air. Fresh air is overrated.' He was well aware he sounded like a grumpy ape.

She didn't answer for a full minute, and Javier was sure she hadn't heard his question since she'd stopped at a white rose bush and bent low to inhale the heady scent. Hell, she even took her time to *caress* a flower. As if she had all the time in the world to stop and smell the roses. He dragged his eyes from her delectable backside as she straightened.

'I used to go for long walks with my mother when I was a child. Sometimes we'd be gone for hours. We'd compete to see who could name the most flowers. I secretly knew she was letting me win more often than not.' The memory brought a sad smile.

It sounded idyllic. The ideal pastime for a perfect princess. Bitterness dredged up his gut. Something must've shown on his face because she swallowed, and let go of the delicate bud.

'So, who does this garden belong to?'

'My mother.'

She stared wide-eyed at him for several heartbeats before her gaze swung to the brownstone. 'Is she here?'

'No. She died five years ago.'

Her green eyes clouded as they returned to him. *'Mi dispiace. Le mie condoglianze.'* Realising she'd spoken her condolences on his loss in her native tongue, she quickly amended. 'I meant—'

'Va bene, dolce principessa, I know what you meant. *Grazie.'*

'Why do you call me that? I'm not a princess.'

'Are you not?'

Her mouth pursed. 'Please don't spoil the moment, Javier.'

He wanted to point out that they weren't having a moment. That he'd chosen this place because it'd been the better alternative to her being spotted in a public park.

The words remained locked in his throat.

Instead he watched her stroll from flower to tree, bench to climbing plant, her shoulders visibly relaxing as she watched a butterfly flit from one petal to the other. He followed her down the stairs to the lower level of the garden, then leaned against an old oak tree as she continued her gentle inspection. She finally sat down at a bench and turned her almost regal face up to the sun. The rays caressed her features, bathing her skin in adoring light. A sight he couldn't pull his gaze from.

'Thank you for bringing me here.'

She didn't see his shrug because her eyes had drifted shut, the delicate lids fluttering. He knew because he was suddenly seated next to her, having had no recollection of moving from the tree.

Sí, he was really losing it.

'De nada,' he murmured, absurdly reluctant to spoil the moment with talk.

Seconds ticked by. His restlessness and bitter frustration abated a touch.

When she smiled, he found his own lips curving in response.

'Your mother must have loved it here. Complete peace in the middle of such a full-on, vibrant city is a rare gift.'

His smile evaporated. 'She...tolerated it. Anywhere that wasn't her home wasn't ever good enough.'

She opened her eyes and glanced at him. Wisps of silkily caramel hair caressed her cheek, and he fought the drive to add his touch to her skin. 'It wasn't enough that *you* were here?' she enquired.

Having asked himself the same question a few disturbingly low times, he should've been prepared for the muffled ache in his chest that had never quite gone away. But hearing the query from her lips sharpened the sting of knowing that he hadn't quite been enough. Nothing and no one had come close to the draw of his mother's dilapidated Northern Spanish home.

He shrugged the pain away, more than a little bewildered at how the conversation had ended up here. How *they* had ended up here. 'She cared for me, in her own way.'

Keen eyes probed. 'But?'

'Anywhere that wasn't Menor Compostela wouldn't have done for her.' Because of one man. And his dangerous influence. An influence that meant his mother hadn't been able to rest in peace even in death.

'Is that where your father is? Menor Compostela?'

'You don't already know this from your little jaunt through my private life?'

Her face clouded. 'I told you, I wasn't the one who dug through your life. My father's my manager. He heard the rumours about our...night together, and probably thought it would be prudent to know—'

'On whom his precious princess had sullied her pristine image?' he finished, renewed bitterness surging high.

'Is that notion so alien to you? Haven't you dug with equal tenacity through my life?'

'Whatever I unearthed hasn't been disclosed to the public, so yes, *chiquita*, I believe I'm above reproach in this instance.' He rose, the illusionary sense of tranquillity gone.

He curbed the bite of regret, more than a little annoyed with himself for the unsettling sensations ricocheting through him.

This day off had been an idiotic idea. Leaving her in his mother's garden, he strode up the steps and entered the empty house.

Javier wasn't sure what he hoped to find inside, but no answers came to him as he walked through rooms with sheet-draped furniture. Everything in here had been new once upon a time, a naïve conviction that granting his mother a fresh start would be what she needed to make a clean break from an unhealthy past.

Nothing he'd done had worked. Bitterness twisted his mouth. Clearly he was extremely ill-equipped to handle or even understand the female psyche.

He would be better off sticking to what he knew best—cut-throat deals and emotionless liaisons.

Except he didn't feel emotionless about one liaison in particular.

Turning away from an expensive entertainment centre his mother had never used to his knowledge, he retraced his steps to the garden.

The sound of her voice stopped him before he rounded a tall rose bush.

'No, I don't want you to come to New York, not if you're going to keep badgering me about this. My mind is made up.' She paused, and Javier heard a muffled voice. Then her breath caught. 'That's all you care about, isn't it? Would it kill you to ask how *I* am?'

Javier's fists curled, the primeval protective instincts that had floored him in the condo returning, stronger than before. About to stride into her presence, he froze as she continued, 'No, Papà, nothing has changed. I'm still taking a break from figure skating. Yes...*indefinitely.*'

The deadly ice in his veins threatened to turn him into a statue. He still managed to move. He must have because she came into view, her eyes growing wide as she tucked her phone into her pocket and drew her arms around her midriff in self-protection. She took a few guarded steps away from him.

Javier was obliquely amused by the useless action. As if anything could save her now. He'd been ready to believe there was some sort of subliminal reason for bringing her to the place he'd built for his mother. Probably because she'd also lost her mother and he'd been seeking some nonexistent connection?

Dios mío. Even the suggestion was unacceptable. He sliced his fingers through his hair. Clearly, he'd been out of his mind.

'Javier?' Her voice held the tiniest wobble.

'Answer me yes or no, Carla. Did you sign our contract knowing you planned to take an indefinite break from ice skating?'

All colour drained from her face, leaving pools of shocked, bottomless moss green. In the deadly stillness, even the insects didn't dare to move. Her lips slowly parted.

Javier braced himself. For what, he wasn't completely sure.

She swallowed hard, the movement echoing through her whole body. Or perhaps she trembled? He didn't care. All he wanted was deliverance from the vacuum of confusion taking hold of him.

'Answer me!'

A short, jerked nod, followed by a simple, 'Yes.'

Absurdly, as he turned away and left his mother's garden, Javier wished she'd lied and answered no.

CHAPTER SEVEN

'SAY SOMETHING. *PER FAVORE,*' Carla whispered. 'Anything. I can't stand the silence.'

They'd left the charming, tranquil garden, and any notion that she was getting to know a much less steel-hearted Javier, far behind. She would never dream of calling him gentle, but the glimpses of the man she'd seen in his mother's garden had touched her heart in a way that had nothing to do with the sexual tension that resided beneath the surface of all their interactions.

That man, if he had existed beyond her imagination, was nowhere to be seen now. The man who grabbed the steering wheel with barely restrained force, whose face was set in a granite mask as he wove through traffic, struck naked apprehension in her heart.

'Javier, please…'

'You weren't planning on telling me until you had your hands on the first quarter's payment.' His voice was conversational, save for the toxic ice that dripped from it. 'I'm guessing the signing bonus wasn't quite enough for you to disappear into the sunset with?'

'No… I mean yes—' She stopped and massaged her temples. 'No, I wasn't planning on disappearing, not without speaking to you first. Not that I was planning to disappear… *Dio, questo è folle.*'

His grating laugh sliced across her every nerve. '*You* think this is insane? Why did you bother even signing a contract with me? With a face and body like yours, you could've landed a number of gullible rich men who would've been only too happy to tolerate a little absence of integrity for a chance to taste what you have to offer.'

His words were a slap that left her reeling, the depth of

her hurt unbelievably deep. 'How dare you? You're being extremely offensive without just cause—'

'*Just cause?* Every interaction I've had with you so far has contained an element of deception on your part.'

'That's not true!'

'Then by all means, Principessa, enlighten me as to where I've misstepped.'

The shivers that had started in the garden rolled over her once more. 'I'd planned to take a break from ice skating, yes, but I hadn't decided exactly when or for how long.'

'And you didn't see fit to inform me of this before you signed on the dotted line? Can you honestly tell me that your decision to keep your plans a secret didn't revolve around the state of your finances?'

'The contract did. Wasn't that the whole point? You told me three years ago you never wanted to see me again. Then all of a sudden you're entertaining an endorsement contract with me? I'm not stupid, Javier. I knew there was a chance this wouldn't be just business—'

'But you entered into the contract anyway?' His lips curled on the words.

'I…hoped you'd moved on. And I planned on fulfilling my part of the deal,' she retorted. 'Because of my wrist I won't be able to compete in two months' time but there are no major championships until next year, so for the sake of your campaign I'll still be number one. I don't know why you're upset with me. Nothing has changed—'

'The insane decision to trust you, professionally, despite your abysmal private life should've been testament to the fact that this deal should never have happened. More fool me, I guess,' he bit out.

They arrived at his Upper East Side building. Far from dissipating, the crowd had only increased in the time they'd been away. Javier's fury congealed as he gunned the car into the garage.

She followed him into the lift, the confined space condensing with nerve-shredding savagery. Unable to keep silent as she was hurled up to what she assumed was her doom, she licked her lips. 'There's something else, Javier.'

Dark brows clamped tight. 'Yes?'

'My father's signed up to write a series of articles for *Vita Italia* magazine.'

'And?' he demanded.

'Technically, it shouldn't have anything to do with my career, but...things haven't been going well between us lately.'

'So he could retaliate against you in the tabloids?'

More miserable than she'd ever thought it was possible to feel, Carla nodded. 'It's worth half a million euros. He won't let it go easily.'

He regarded her for several tense seconds. The lift pinged open and still he stared at her. 'What a tangled mess you've woven yourself into, Principessa,' he finally mused.

Exiting, he strode for the double doors leading to the penthouse.

She reached him just as he threw the door open. Desperate, she grabbed his arm. 'Javier—'

In an agile move she wouldn't have attributed to a powerfully built man such as him, he slammed the door shut and pinned her against it. His hands circled her arms, his body caging hers with predatory precision. 'Even if I chose to believe that you coming clean now isn't a clever plot to save yourself from being sued for breach of contract, it doesn't excuse you from keeping your plans from me,' he sliced at her.

This close, she could see the gold flecks overlaid on the mahogany of his eyes, harshly beautiful and completely captivating. She stared up at him, until his accusation dripped into her mind. 'You plucked me from hospital and brought me here, then left me to my own devices for two weeks. Even if I'd come to any concrete decision—which I haven't— today would've been my first chance to tell you.'

The hands shackling her arms skated over her shoulders and up the sides of her neck to rest at her nape. Heat dragged through her at the electrifying skin contact. She rejected the melting sensation racing through her body as his thumbs rested over her twin pulses.

'You play the aggrieved damsel so well,' he murmured, his breath washing over her face. 'But if you'd thought about anyone but yourself you'd have made sure that you and I weren't once again in this position.'

'And what position would that be? Me, once again appealing to your better nature and you determined to believe the absolute worst of me? Let me guess, you're going to fire me now?'

He stepped closer, bringing his body a scant inch from hers. The lethal power whipping through him and her own body's brazen excitement robbed her of breath.

'You would love that, wouldn't you? Another salacious piece of gossip for your fans to scavenge over? Is this how we're destined to interact? You inviting trouble my way every time?'

'I don't mean to,' she murmured back, her attention absorbed by the unique bruised-rose shade of his lips. The insane urge to trace the shape with her fingers was so strong she couldn't suppress the moan that rose from her soul.

His eyes darkened, his breath hissing out at the revealing sound.

'You don't mean to. And yet here we are.'

'End this, then. Fire me,' she urged.

'No.' His head descended a fraction. 'If I fire you, you'll no longer be mine to command. You'll be free to wreak your havoc on someone else.'

'So you're doing mankind a favour?'

'*Sí*, that is exactly right.'

Another inch closer and she felt the full impact of his body. Right down to the unmistakeable arousal imprinted against her belly. The vivid memory of his power inside her scorched her senses. Her nipples peaked, the sensitive buds demanding shockingly immediate appeasement.

She squirmed, her body's uncontrollable craving almost overpowering her. He moved with her, a subtle roll of his hips, a teasing slide of one broad thumb across her lower lip.

Her limbs weakened. 'Javier.' Her voice was a husky plea, either to end the torture or to satisfy it.

'You want me,' he stated, his voice deep and sure with masculine confidence.

Heat rushed into her face, ramping her temperature even higher. She wanted to look away, to deny the taunting words. But she couldn't pull her gaze from the hunger and sensual promise in his eyes.

'Do you want me to kiss you, Carla *mia*? Are you hoping perhaps that your body can achieve what your character has failed to do so far and pull me into your web?'

A part of her mourned that he would never see past the desperate misunderstanding of three years ago. But the greater part of her just wanted to experience the hot, erotic skill of his kiss.

Senses clamouring, she threw caution to the wind, her head moving in a nod before she'd fully computed her actions and the inevitable repercussions. 'Yes, I want you to kiss me.'

A muffled sound that could've been a curse or a prayer ripped from his lips. In the next breath, his mouth slanted over hers. The last vestiges of sanity ripped free, her senses plunging into free fall as pure sensation took over. Flames licked at each point of contact, which was pretty much everywhere from their fused lips to the masculine thighs tangling with hers. But the sensation of his tongue sliding against hers was what had her gasping in delight, the concentrated pleasure arrowing straight between her legs to the place only he had ever owned.

She whimpered, her bound hand sliding around his waist, holding on for dear life as he explored her with a thoroughness that seared her deeper than she'd ever been touched. Her other hand wandered up his tight body, over hard contours and heated flesh to the silky waves of his hair. A wicked memory impinged, and she fisted the luxurious strands. Javier jerked against her, a growl erupting between their lips as his erection jumped against her belly.

One hand cupped her breast, catching the stiff peak between his fingers for a delicious pull that made her groan. His other hand gripped her waist tight and lifted her off the floor. 'Put your legs around me,' he commanded.

Complying brought her most sensitive part flush against him. Striding sure and swift as if she weighed nothing, he entered the living room and laid her down on the sofa.

Slow, lingering kisses trailed from her jaw, along her collarbone to her shoulder. She tried to caress him in turn and was confronted with one immobilised hand. Frustration clawed through her...at the overabundance of clothes between them, the slow pace of his attention. With the hand still in his hair, she attempted to draw him closer, deepen the kiss. He let her have the lead, until the need for air forced her to break away.

He laughed at the rapid rise and fall of her chest.

'So needy, Principessa. Was your last boyfriend not up to the task of satisfying you? Don't worry. When I make you mine again, that memory will fade away for ever.' He started to curl his hand around her thigh.

She froze in degrees, her head battling hard with her senses as the reality of what was happening dawned on her.

When I make you mine.

There would be no charm offensive involved this time round, no drive in his sports car and laughter on a beach underpinning the sexual intent in each glance and each word.

Unlike Miami three years ago, what would happen here would be a vengeful taking, fuelled by Javier's belief that she had wronged him. Again. Desire still wove like a lingering drug in her bloodstream, but Carla unclenched her fist from his hair, ignoring her screaming senses. She couldn't let this go any further. Her vulnerability when it came to

Javier was shamefully evident in the way she was sprawled beneath him with only the clothes on her body barring her need from him.

'Don't tell me the *principessa* has remembered that she's once again cavorting with someone beneath her regard?'

She met his gaze, forcing herself to see past the mockery and acid-dipped words to the hurt and pain beneath.

'What did it do, Javier?' she ventured, hoping for a straight answer this time.

Dark-lashed eyes narrowed. *'Perdón?'*

'That statement about your parentage. What exactly was the damage from it?'

He tensed, his face tautening into an implacable mask. 'If you're trying to get on my good side, this isn't the way to go about it.'

'Please. I'm just trying to understand why you hate me so much.'

He vaulted off her, his breath escaping in harsh exhalations. Locks of hair hung in unruly waves, but even that dishevelled look lent him a rakish air that threatened to reignite her thawing senses.

Sitting up, she swung her legs to the floor and kept them firmly, unwillingly closed. She watched him stride to the drinks cabinet and pour himself a stiff drink. Tossing it back, he poured a glass of water and returned to set it down on the table next to her.

All without speaking.

She sighed. 'Clearly something happened to make all this torturing of me necessary. The least you can do is tell me the reason for my suffering.'

A harsh bark of laughter cracked across the room. 'You think *you're* suffering?'

She caught his meaning when her gaze dropped below his belt. Her blush was furnace-hot and deeply embarrassing. 'You know what I mean.'

He sliced his hand through his hair, unsettling the strands

even more. 'And you think understanding where I'm coming from will free you to give yourself permission to accept my touch?' he snarled.

'Why do you act as if I've treated you like a leper?'

His smile was terse and cruel. 'You were singularly memorable in your urgency to get away from me the morning after we had sex, *querida*.'

She shook her head. 'I can tell you until I'm hoarse that I slept with you because I wanted to. I just didn't deal very well with the aftermath. And you're changing the subject.' She firmed her voice, meeting his blazing gaze without flinching.

Slowly he sauntered towards her. Instead of taking the seat next to her, he sat down on the large teak coffee table that complemented the rest of the earth-toned, conceptually stunning décor. His thighs braced on either side of hers, he leaned forward on his elbows, another hard smile showcasing his impressive cheekbones. 'You want to know what havoc your father's little digging expedition wreaked?'

She held firm and nodded.

'Muy bien,' he grunted. 'My mother was seventeen and on her way to church one day when she caught the eye of a rich man in his fancy car. To most people that sounds like the beginning of a fairy tale. From my mother, it was the beginning of the end, only she didn't know it at the time. She'd led a strict, sheltered life and had no idea she'd caught the eye of the son of the baron from the neighbouring town. A *married* son of a baron twice her age. He seduced her, alienated her from her family, who eventually disowned her, and set her up in a run-down house on the edge of his estate. That was where I was born six years later. I was delivered by a retired midwife because my father didn't want anyone to know he'd fathered a bastard, which was a standing joke because everyone knew, of course.'

Carla's chest tightened at the pain etched on his face.

'There were complications with my birth. My mother

survived, but she was never completely whole. She should have been in a hospital with medical professionals not in a shack with an old woman to birth me.' The hands dangling between his legs tightened into hard fists. 'I grew up knowing he was the man who had wilfully sacrificed my mother's health on the altar of his reputation. Unfortunately, that wasn't the only unsavoury trait he possessed. He strung my mother along with the usual empty promise to leave his baroness for her, even while *she* supplied him with heirs and spares on a regular basis.'

'So you have half-brothers and sisters?'

One masculine eyebrow cocked. 'Of course not. I don't exist, remember?'

She flinched, and barely resisted the urge to touch him. 'You exist. If to no one else you must have done to your mother.'

'She home schooled me at his insistence—private school was never on the cards on account of his many children needing his every euro. I was only allowed to play in the garden of the house. While boys my age were bonding over football, I wasn't even allowed to climb a tree in case I hurt myself and I had to suffer the presence of the village doctor.'

Tears stung her eyes. She blinked them away quickly before he spotted the helpless empathy that blazed in her heart for him. Just for something to do, she picked up her water glass and took a sip, her heart tripping frantically as he continued.

'The upside of all that cloistered existence was that I excelled academically. If nothing else, she was quietly proud of me for not letting her down the way my father had.'

'Did she ever leave him?'

A haunted smile touched his lips, as if he was caught in a despondent memory. 'I bought her several homes around the world, had the best horticulturists recreate her beloved garden in each home. She didn't stay in any property for more than a few weeks, a month at most. It was almost as if she couldn't physically stand to be away from that godfor-saken ramshackle house, waiting for that bastard to spare her a crumb of his time.' His voice was an edgy sneer, his jaw clenched tight.

'Did you two ever interact?'

'I didn't actually *see* him up close until I was nine years old. I broke my boundaries and snuck off to the big castle on the hill—it was surprisingly easy. I hid in the bushes and watched him playing tennis with one of his other children. I wanted to walk up to him, announce who I was and spit in his face for making my mother cry late at night when she thought I was asleep.'

A light shudder quivered through him and she knew he was caught up in memory. This time, she ventured a light touch.

The moment her fingers grazed his knuckles, he jerked away. Springing to his feet, he paced to the window. Carla curled her fingers, berating herself for being hurt by his rejection when all the hurt in this situation belonged to him.

'I managed to get myself a scholarship to university a year early. He turned up the day before I left, mistakenly think-ing the coast was clear. I finally got a chance to give him a big piece of my mind. The next time we met was when I returned to Menor Compostela after my mother died.' His mouth tightened for several tense seconds. 'Her last wish was to be buried within her family crypt. I guess in death she wanted to belong somewhere. But they refused. My fa-ther has the power to overrule their decision.'

'But to do that he has to publicly acknowledge his asso-ciation with her?'

'*Sí,*' he breathed unevenly. 'He refused to help. Until three years ago.'

Dread liquidised her insides. 'What happened?'

'His grapes were wiped out by freak weather a week be-fore the harvest. He lost millions of euros' worth of stock overnight. His Rioja had been producing mediocre wine due to bad management for years anyway, and he was on the verge of bankruptcy. Had it been left to me, I would've happily watched him sink into the mud he valued over my mother's life,' he grated icily.

'But you stepped in?'

'On condition he did the right thing by my mother.'

Foreboding gripped Carla's nape. The bleak landscape he'd painted required no maps as to how the story ended. She wanted to tell him to stop, to forgive her guilt by association. But Javier was ruthlessly laying out the full picture. Helplessly she stared at him, bearing the full brunt of his complete condemnation.

'The tabloid quote about my bastard parentage was printed three days after I saved his precious estate. It's one thing to have your secrets whispered behind your back. As long as no one dared to confront him with the truth, he could pretend he was a pillar of society. The potential for outing a dirty little secret prompted other journalists to dig even deeper. My mother, finally accepting he would never do right by her, had got her own back by listing him as the father of her child once she knew she was dying. Someone got hold of my birth certificate and it was suddenly all over the news. He refused to take my calls for two years.'

She flicked her tongue over suddenly dry lips. 'Javier, I'm so very sorry.'

He strode back to where she sat. One falsely indolent hand tucked a wisp of hair behind her ear before his flat eyes scoured her from forehead to chin and back again.

'You probably are, *querida*. But the reality is my mother is still buried in that back yard I detested all my life because that is where she *settled* for when she knew she couldn't be with her family. I watched her *settle* for less than she was worth all her life. I have no room in my life now for forgiveness. Not until I make things right for her.' His eyes slowly narrowed. 'And you throwing obstacles in my way hasn't helped my disposition one little bit.'

Her breath shuddered out. She opened her mouth, to say what, she didn't know.

He rose abruptly, strangling any response she might have thought of. When she realised he was heading for the front door, she regained her power of speech.

'Where are you going?'

He flicked the keys he'd plucked up from a nearby console. 'This day off has turned out to be a terrible idea.'

'You're going into the office?'

'Yes. For one thing, I need to deal with the fire your father started.'

A wave of relief swept through her. 'You're stopping the *Vita Italia* articles?'

'Unless he's prepared to prove to me that there's nothing damaging to you in them, they will never see the light of day. Not unless he relishes opposing me in court. I hope he doesn't. My tolerance levels are stretched thin as it is.'

'What about your father?'

'His grapes are failing again. I just need to bide my time.'

He gripped the door handle and turned before she summoned her voice once more. 'And what about me, Javier?'

He turned with a lithe grace that was sublime to watch. Dark eyes raked her from head to toe, returning to hers far more intense than they'd been a few minutes ago. 'Patience, Principessa,' he murmured. 'I'll get round to dealing with you sooner than you think.'

He was gone before she'd exhaled her next breath. Like a deflated balloon, she sagged onto the sofa. When she managed to get her reeling senses under control, she pulled her legs to her chest and replayed everything Javier had said to her.

Cradling her chin on her knees, she closed her eyes in despair.

No wonder he'd been furious with her. It didn't matter that the major fault was her father's. Between the two of

them, they'd denied Javier the one thing he craved most—
peace for his mother.

She couldn't do anything about it now, the harm was
done. But she could see to it that her father got the message
about her life being her own from now on, once and for all.
Heading to her suite, she located her phone and dialled his
number. She let it go to voicemail three times before she
finally left a message. Her father would answer her summons, or face the lawyers she intended to hire on Monday.

As for Javier, she prayed that, when the time came, whatever punishment he chose to dole out would be tempered
with the same consideration that had prompted him to take
her to his mother's secluded garden.

CHAPTER EIGHT

SHE SAW JAVIER for fleeting periods over the weekend, the last being an abrupt greeting and goodbye at the door on Sunday night when he told her he had a meeting in Los Angeles the next morning and would be gone for two days.

Slotting the mild bereft ache in her chest under the firm heading of listlessness during his absence, she gathered the product information Darren had provided and parked herself in the window seat of the living room. A glance down to the street showed the crowd that had been thinning over the weekend had finally dispersed.

Breathing easier, she made plans to go for a walk after lunch, and opened the pack.

The full-page, colour headshot of Javier stopped her breath. He was staring straight into the camera, the cobalt blue of his open-necked shirt making his eyes reflect a lighter bronze shade than their normal mahogany. His captivating mouth was trapped in the beginnings of a smile that promised charm and sin, his stubbled jaw and strong throat completing a heart-stopping package that absorbed her attention for much longer than she deemed wise. It was only when she realised her lungs were burning from holding in her breath that she impatiently roused herself from her lust-drenched stupor.

He was just a man.

A complex, dynamic man who it turned out was just as prone to human vulnerabilities as the next person.

But it doesn't make him less fascinating to you. Quite the opposite.

She flipped the page over, irritated with herself for her inability to stop thinking about Javier. The next page gave a brief history of J Santino Inc. Javier had started out as a corporate investor barely out of college. But his love for the finer things in life and a keen eye for design had seen him branch out into luxury-goods marketing by the time he was twenty-five. He'd added a late design degree and started the J Santino product range. Carla knew that the overnight success most people attributed to people like Javier was the product of hard, relentless work. But for a man like Javier, the burning desire to succeed had been born from the circumstances of his life. He'd wanted to rise above the label placed on him in his mother's womb.

Her heart squeezed and she fought the urge to turn back the page and glance at his picture once more. Instead she moved on, familiarising herself with the fascinating history behind Javier's latest launch.

He hadn't been joking when he'd referred to her tequila excess that night three years ago. What he didn't know was that she'd overheard him talking to Draco about his love for the liquor, and, feeling bold and rebellious, had decided to try it for herself. She'd been fascinated with the smoothness of the spirit and the heat that burned through her, just as she'd been fascinated with the man who'd instigated a similar heat inside her.

The rest had been history...

Or not.

She finished reading and checked her phone and email, her heart squeezing with dread and disappointment to see nothing from her father. This was rougher, uncharted territory for them, one she didn't think would get easier seeing as her father obviously didn't want to take the amicable route.

Restless and angsty, she tugged on her ankle boots. She didn't exactly feel cooped up in the apartment, but, with Felipe the butler also off for the day, the continued silence was beginning to get to her. Plus she couldn't walk past the sofa without reliving the heated moments she'd shared with

Javier, and that was wrecking her concentration. Another glance down to the street showed it was still clear.

Going to her room, she pulled a cashmere jumper over her top and brushed out her hair before pulling a stylish cap over it. Locating her sunglasses, she slipped them on and grabbed her handbag. In the foyer, she smiled at Johnny, the concierge manager, then froze as her way was blocked by a giant of a man with a crew cut and a muscle-bound body straining in a three-piece suit.

'Morning, Miss Nardozzi,' the giant greeted her.

Her smile slipped a notch. 'Morning. Umm, I'm sorry, do I know you?'

'No. We haven't been introduced yet. I'm Antonio, your minder. Mr Santino asked me to ensure you aren't disturbed if you decide to leave the building.'

Carla wasn't sure which emotion surged higher— irritation at Javier's blithe domination of her life, or the un-wanted gladdening of her heart that he was looking out for her.

Or perhaps she was deluding herself entirely by assum-ing the latter scenario. Javier had left her with little doubt that he intended to keep pursuing reparations for the wrong done to him. He didn't trust her. Antonio's presence was a bracing reminder of that. Perhaps he expected her to run away while he was in LA.

Her smile melting off her face, she glanced at the body-guard. 'I'm going for a walk. I have no idea how long I'll be.'

'Not a problem. You won't even know I'm there.'

Resisting the very unladylike urge to snort her disbelief, she exited into the sunshine, digging out her phone as she hit the sidewalk.

I don't need a bodyguard, grazie. I'm perfectly capable of ensuring my own safety so you can call him off now.

The reply came within seconds.

Since you've met him, I'm assuming you're no longer in the penthouse. He stays. And don't think about sending him away. He answers to only me.

She gritted her teeth.

This is unacceptable.

Your safety is non-negotiable. He stays. And, Principessa…

I told you not to call me that!

Any stunts you attempt to pull will be answered with equal punishment.

You're thousands of miles away. What's the worst you can do?

Try me.

Eye-roll.

Attempt that when I'm standing in front of you.

Double eye-roll.

Your fearlessness is commendable. If extremely foolhardy. Eat something, Principessa. You'll need your strength to repeat this feat of daring you're suddenly brazen enough to attempt.

Bring it.

Carla realised she was grinning as she stopped at a crossing. Curious glances from strangers had her straightening her features as she crossed the street onto Fifth Avenue. The sights and sounds of New York City buffeted her as she walked in the spring sunshine. On impulse, she stepped into an exclusive boutique of a designer whose work she was familiar with. She browsed until Antonio's solid presence outside the door began to draw attention. Smiling at the attendants, she quickly exited only to stop outside when her phone rang.

Her heart performed a crazy somersault, but the number displayed on her screen wasn't familiar. Or the one she'd texted Javier with minutes ago.

'Hello?'

'Hi, Carla, it's Darren.'

Her stomach dipped. Swallowing what she refused to acknowledge was disappointment, she injected lightness into her tone. '*Ciao*, how can I help you?'

'I know Javier is out of town, but I'll be scouting the three nightclubs we shortlisted for the shoot tonight, and wondered whether you'd like to come along. The earlier we nail it down, the quicker we can move things along.'

Carla opened her mouth, an automatic refusal rising out of habit. Socialising for anything but her career had been struck off her list after her one and only life-changing time in Miami. But slowly, she closed her mouth. The idea of spending another evening alone in the penthouse drew a grimace. Besides, this wasn't really socialising. It was work-related.

'Uh… Carla?'

'*Sì*, I'm here. I don't know much about nightclubs, but I'd like to come along.'

'Great! I'll swing by and pick you up at seven? We can get something to eat beforehand if you want?'

Eat something, Principessa.

'I want. I'll see you at seven.'

She hung up with a different smile on her face. The break for independence was a tiny one, but it felt good. She glanced at her phone again, her smile dimming at the thought of her father.

Pressing the buttons, she dialled.

He answered after several long rings. 'What do you want?'

A cloud floated past the sun, echoing her mood as her chest tightened. 'You know what this is about. I've left you several messages.'

'You can't summon me like a lapdog. You forget who is the father and who is the child here.'

'I just want to talk, Papà. Find a way to resolve this.'

He laughed, an overloud, slurred rumble that made her frown. 'Are you drunk?'

'Watch yourself, *ragazza*. You may think you suddenly hold all the cards, but I'm not averse to bringing you down a peg or two.'

'What's that supposed to mean?'

'It means call off Santino and whatever plans he has of sticking his nose in where it doesn't belong, or...'

Her stomach hollowed. 'Or, what?'

'Or I'll give a different kind of interview. One he won't have the power to stop. You want to know how your mother died? I've tried to spare you the gory details, for your own sake, but if you really want to know, I'll tell you when I'm ready. Or you can find out about it at some point in the future. Either way, I hope you're as strong enough to take the truth as you insist you are.'

'What? Papà—' Her words echoed down a disconnected line. Chills rippled over her. She didn't realise she'd stumbled to a halt on the sidewalk until Antonio cleared his throat.

'Miss, is everything okay?'

She forced life into her feet, her steps growing faster as she spotted Javier's apartment building. She crossed the foyer without looking up and was shaking by the time she let herself back into the penthouse. Her ringing phone a second later made her jump.

Hands trembling, she answered it.

'What's wrong?' Javier demanded.

'What...how do you know—?'

'Tell me,' Javier commanded.

'My father... I just spoke to him...' She shook her head to clear it, to find a way to attribute the conversation with her father to anything other than a clear threat. A threat not born in her wildest imagination.

'And?'

She clamped her mouth shut, the thick cord of guilt she'd never been able to loosen from her heart tightening even further.

'Carla.' Javier growled a warning.

'Please... I'm fine...'

A thick curse ripped through her senses. 'What did he say to you?'

'Did you stop the articles in *Vita Italia*?' she countered.

'Yes. I told you I was going to. I wasn't satisfied with some of the subject matters.'

Dread raked her stomach. 'I need you to lay off my father, Javier. Please. Until I talk to him again.'

'No. Tell me what he's up to and I'll deal with it.'

'No, questo è il mio problema. Io ne occupo io, non tu.'

'I find it adorable that you slip into Italian when you're fired up, Principessa, but you're wrong. This is not just your problem. I hate to break it to you if you haven't already worked it out, but your father is operating from a place of pure greed, just like my father when it suits him. And I guarantee that every misguided decision he makes from now on will impact both of us.'

'So you're helping me to fight him?'

'In this case, protecting you from him also protects my brand, so yes. Now, tell me what he said to you,' he insisted for the third time.

'He said something, about...my mother. H-how she died.'

'How did she die?'

Debilitating pain deadened her limbs. She stumbled to the sofa and dropped into it. 'That's just it. I don't know. I wasn't there, and he won't tell me. But I know whatever happened, it had something to do with me.'

'How is that possible?' he demanded.

'It sounds absurd, I know, but, whatever it is, I can't find out any other way, Javier. Please. Give me time to deal with him my way.'

A harsh exhalation. 'Sorry, *querida*, I can make no promises.'

'Javier!'

For the second time in the space of half an hour, Carla was confronted with a disconnected line.

Rushing to her room, she located her laptop and opened up her email. Typing without the full use of all her fingers was frustrating in the extreme.

My full and final offer—thirty percent of the endorsement proceeds, and the Tuscany villa, in return for the truth about Mamma, and no press involvement. Also, you will no longer be my manager.

She and her father would never have a proper familial relationship. She was better off accepting it now and walking away, no matter much her heart shredded at the thought. Shaking, she pressed send to her father's private email address, finally accepting that this was her only option if she wanted to draw a line under the acrimony they'd been living with for years.

She held her breath until she received notification that he'd opened it.

His response came within minutes. It reeked with a smugness that made her stomach turn.

Agreed. But I need the first payment within the next fourteen days.

Fine.

She closed her laptop, a wave of despair gripping her. She'd just negotiated her way out of her father's life. She blinked away the tears that formed and straightened her spine. For years she'd yearned for a father who loved her. Today, she needed to accept that would never happen. For some reason, he was incapable of it.

She paced the penthouse for a full hour trying to come up with a cogent solution. She'd bought herself some time, but the next endorsement payment wouldn't be for another two months.

Her heart broke as she settled on her next-best option. A quick call later and her mother's beloved cottage was listed with the estate agent. Praying it was only a stopgap measure she wouldn't need to use, Carla undressed and went into the bathroom to shower. Careful to keep her cast out of the spray, she shampooed her hair one-handed, the arduous task taking her mind off her turbulent thoughts.

It worked until she turned off the shower, then the memories from three years ago flooded back.

The training for the championship that had taken her away from Tuscany for several weeks. Her row with her father when she'd asked for some time off before the championship. Her appeal to her mother to intervene. Her time in Miami. Her father unexpectedly absenting himself from the tournament afterwards. His equally sudden return for the ceremony of her being crowned champion. His cold announcement that her mother was dead. And his unequivocal refusal to discuss how she'd died.

Carla shuddered, her skin clammy in the vast room where she stood in only a towel. Despite what the death certificate had said, she'd never managed to rid herself of the suspicion that there was more to her mother's death than she'd been made privy to.

Her father's thinly veiled comments over the years had only fed that suspicion.

The idea that he would make public whatever secret surrounded her mother's death threatened to rip her in two. Javier had intimated that she was feeding the monster by giving in to her father. But the alternative was worse. She couldn't let her mother's memory be dragged through the mires of social media for the sake of financial gain. The knowledge that it was her own father making that threat wounded her deep and long, but she would suffer it. For the sake of the mother who had loved her for as long as she could.

Firm-jawed, she dried herself and went into her closet. Vast amounts of white dominated her wardrobe.

Deliberately bypassing the white, she reached into the corner of her closet and dragged out a pair of black leather pants, a gold-threaded black top she'd never worn because the cut had been too risqué and studded black boots. She pulled the top on, her face flaming slightly at the thought of going out without a bra. Catching her hair up, she secured it with a diamond pin that had belonged to her mother. Then she went to town with her make-up.

Where she'd only worn the very lightest shades and gloss, she brushed on smoky eye shadow, cheekbone-enhancing blush, and dark red gloss over her lips.

The end result was dramatic enough to stop her breath. Before the tiny speck of doubt could take hold and ruin her night out, she snatched up her gold lamé clutch and transferred her phone and personal items into it.

The sound of the buzzer brought the relief and shameless inevitability she needed. Answering it, she finished her ensemble with a leather jacket and left the penthouse.

Darren's double take once she exited the lift buoyed her confidence and she smiled as she crossed the foyer.

'Wow, you look amazing!'

'*Grazie,*' she murmured. 'You don't look so bad yourself.'

'What, this?' He indicated his dark grey button-down shirt, black chinos, and the black jacket he wore over it. 'It's okay, but hardly the cutting edge of fashion. Not that you're not worth going cutting edge for,' he quickly amended. 'I meant, I prefer to dazzle a woman with my wit, not my attire.'

She laughed, a little of her churning emotions subsiding under the easy banter. He escorted her outside, then glanced over his shoulder. 'Umm...will that BFG be accompanying us everywhere tonight?'

Carla grimaced. 'He's harmless... I think. And barely noticeable once you get used to him.' She looked over her shoulder and smiled at Antonio. He cracked a return smile.

'Right. O...kay,' Darren responded, his tone a little bewildered. 'I'm cool with it if you are. The restaurant is a couple of blocks away.' He glanced at her heeled boots. 'You don't mind walking, do you?'

'Not at all.' She smiled and received a quick, appreciative one back. They fell into an easy stride, the conversation light and casual. It continued through a delicious meal at an Irish-themed bar and restaurant then out onto an even busier Manhattan street. 'The first club is Downtown. I have VIP passes.' He hailed a cab and helped her into it. Antonio took residence in the front seat, his burly presence making the cab driver blink hard before shrugging in defeat. Darren raised his eyebrows at her, and Carla couldn't help but giggle.

Outside the exclusive Cuban nightclub, limos competed with flashy sports cars for attention. They were shown to a VIP section with plush gold velvet sofas and an unlimited supply of complimentary drinks. Vowing to stick to a two-drink threshold, Carla sipped her first drink slowly. Their easy conversation continued with Darren regaling her with stories of his childhood in Dublin. When the club owner came over to speak to him, she took off her jacket and went down to the edge of the dance floor. She smiled noncommittally at a few interested glances, resolutely ignored the more pointed ones, then sighed in relief when Darren joined her a few minutes later.

'So what do you think?' He gestured to the club's interior and dance floor.

The rich, slightly ethnic theme was sensual enough to evoke the spirit of Javier's brand, while contemporary enough to appeal to the sophisticated urbanite.

She smiled. 'I like the music, and I think the space will work well.' During dinner, he'd expanded on the brief of *work hard, play harder* theme of the shoot, with the primary shoot being on the ice rink and the secondary at the nightclub.

Darren's hand slid around her waist. 'Want to try it out?' He grinned.

Shrugging, she nodded. 'Why not?'

They descended into the crowd to the tune of throbbing Cuban drums.

Laughing, she entered the fray, throwing her arms above her head partly to keep her wrist from being accidentally re-injured. Darren, a more than adequate partner, stayed close, his appreciative gaze dancing over her body every now and then. After two songs, the tempo changed to a slower, sexier beat. Darren danced closer, but still kept a respectable distance. Catching her forearms, he gently placed them on his shoulders, a small smile playing at his lips as he swayed in time with her.

'You really are stunningly beautiful, you know that?' he confessed in her ear.

She blushed, wishing away the sudden embarrassment and the slight discomfiting realisation that perhaps he was more interested in her than he'd let on. 'Umm…*grazie*,' she murmured.

He laughed, the careful hands he'd placed on her waist drawing her closer. 'I love your accent. In fact I don't think there's a single thing about you that I don't find—' He froze suddenly, his eyes bulging as he swallowed hard. 'Oh, hell,' he muttered.

She blinked in surprise. 'What's wrong?'

'Carla.'

Her head whipped round at the barely repressed violence in the deep, low voice that curled over her shoulder.

Javier stood three scant feet away, his nostrils flared in volcanic fury as he stared at them. His chest rose and fell in rapid rhythm, his fists clenched at his sides. The emotions vibrating off him lent him an impossibly overwhelming aura, a fact that transmitted to the nearest clubbers, who'd stopped dancing and were openly staring.

Alarmed at his unexpected presence, she went to step away and stumbled. Darren's hold tightened on her.

The growl that rose over the music had several people stepping away, more than a few of them making room and nudging each other as the threat of a salacious confrontation thickened in the air.

'What are you doing here?' she croaked.

He didn't answer. His gaze remained fixed with naked intensity on where Darren's hands rested on her waist. 'If you value the use of your limbs, O'Hare, I suggest you remove your hands from her body. Right now.'

Darren released her with comic swiftness. 'Mr Santino—'

'Leave. Now.'

Outrage sparked within her. 'Javier! You can't do that—'

'Take *your* hands off the man, Carla, so he can leave, or I won't be responsible for what happens next,' he snarled with a guttural tone that was barely coherent.

But she got the message.

She took her time, though, despite the quaking unfolding alongside the outrage, because she refused to be intimidated. Darren stepped away, his apprehension escalating as he swallowed hard again. He attempted to cast her an apologetic glance. Javier took a single step towards him and he changed his mind, turning in the opposite direction to disappear through the seething crowd.

Javier turned his bristling frame to her. 'You have two minutes,' he bit out.

She raised one brow, unwilling to admit the blood strumming urgently through her veins was in any way to do with his sudden dramatic appearance. That would hand him too much power over her. 'Two minutes for what?'

'To retrieve whatever you came here with. Or we leave without it.'

'What makes you think I'm going anywhere with you?' she challenged.

His eyes gleamed. 'Principessa, for once in your life, do what is best for you. You do not want to test me right now. I can guarantee you that. You certainly don't want to do it here, in full view of your captive audience.'

A quick glance around showed they'd drawn even more interested glances now Darren had scurried away. Thankfully, the club had a 'no photography' policy, but that didn't mean their every move wasn't being recorded by security cameras.

'They're not staring at me. You're the one making a spectacle of yourself.'

Once again he didn't respond. She got the distinct impression he was holding onto his control by the thinnest thread. The staring contest lasted a full minute.

Then, blood roaring in her ears—with embarrassment only, she was sure—Carla walked off the dance floor and climbed the steps to the VIP area. Antonio handed over her clutch and jacket, then stepped forward to make room as they left the club.

Supremely conscious of Javier's seething presence behind her, she could barely walk and was thankful when they emerged into fresh air.

She immediately struck out for the busy intersection three blocks away. Less than a handful of steps later, Javier stepped firmly into her path. 'Where the hell do you think you're going?' His voice was a razor-sharp blade, lethal and unmistakeable in the semi-darkness.

'I told you I'm not going anywhere with you.'

'Think again.'

'Do me a favour, Javier, and leave me the hell alone!' She whirled round and tore blindly down a side street.

She noticed two things mere seconds into her flight. One, the alley was smoky and dark with a single yellow bulb strung high above their heads. Two, it terminated in a dead-end a few hundred feet away. She heard Javier snarl a *do not disturb* instruction to Antonio before his sure, measured footsteps echoed between her frantic ones. A dozen feet from the sheer wall soaring high in front of her, she turned and stood her ground.

He stalked closer, his dark clothes lending him an air of unbridled masculinity and danger.

Despite herself, she shivered. 'You don't frighten me, Santino.'

He laughed. 'I know I don't. But we both know why you're running. Rest easy, *chiquita*, you're in luck. I'm in the mood to give you exactly what you want.'

CHAPTER NINE

JAVIER'S EYES NARROWED on her, his senses still grappling with the changes in the woman standing in front of him. Perhaps it was the rage boiling his blood that had him so unbalanced. Or the flaying alarm that had gripped him when he'd returned to the penthouse and found her gone. Either way, he straddled the very edge of control as he watched her sassy mouth tighten.

'As usual, I have no idea what you're talking about. I don't care for whatever it is you think I'm in the mood for.'

'What the hell are you wearing?' he sliced at her, his gaze taking in the dramatic beauty of her face, the shiny leather hugging her hips and thighs, and the top that was slashed in too many provocative places to require a bra. The transformation from innocent to sultry siren was playing holy havoc with a libido he'd spent the last forty-eight hours battling. And failing.

'They're called clothes, Javier,' she threw back at him.

He stalked closer. She retreated. Her back touched the damp wall and she froze.

He consciously unclenched his fingers and sucked in a sustaining breath. 'I returned home to find you gone. No note. No phone call. Had it not been for Antonio, I wouldn't have had a clue where you were. And when I find you, you give me *attitude*?'

Her eyes sparked in the dim light. 'You hung up on me mid-conversation. What did you expect, that I would be curled up in a ball of misery, crying my eyes out?'

'I was in the middle of a meeting when we talked. I rearranged my schedule and took the rest of the meeting on my flight back from LA. If you'd bothered to answer me when

I called you back once my meeting ended, we could've finished our conversation.'

She frowned. 'I got no call from you.'

'I landed three hours ago. Check your phone.'

Rebellion blazed for a second before she dug through her tiny bag. She activated it, her eyes widening a touch. 'I was in the nightclub. I didn't hear it.'

'Clearly. You were too busy on the dance floor, running away from your problems by rubbing yourself against the first available guy. I'm flattened by the overwhelming sense of déjà vu.'

'I wasn't rubbing myself against Darren! We were working on your precious campaign. And even if we weren't, what's it to you? So what if maybe I wanted to spread my wings a little? Does it state in my contract that I have to remain celibate while performing my duties to the almighty Javier Santino? No, it doesn't.'

He stiffened, pure hellfire rushing through him. 'You were planning on *sleeping with him*?'

Heat stormed into her face. 'That's none of your business. But of course that doesn't matter to you, does it? You just had to step in and ruin my fun.'

He closed the gap between them, physically unable to stop himself from reaching for her. '*Fun?* Is that what you were looking for? You want to spread your wings sexually? Is that it?' he muttered, each word he spoke lancing him hard and merciless. The idea that she would do this in his absence, invite another man's hands on her body, ripped a path of insanity through his brain.

'N...no, not exactly.'

Javier didn't hear her. His attention was wholly absorbed by the delectable gleam of her red-glossed lips, the memory of their taste as intoxicating to his senses as the most potent spirit. His hands slid from her shoulders down her torso, his fingers easily spanning her trim waist. He jerked her to him, and slanted his mouth over hers before he had time to think.

His kiss was hard, a merciless punishment for every frame of what he'd seen when he walked into the nightclub, every moment he'd wasted thinking of her, reliving her desperate pain after her father's phone call, and the helplessness he'd experienced from three thousand miles away. Hell, he'd even gone so far as to wonder if he'd overblown the events of the morning after their night together in Miami and she hadn't actually acted that badly.

And all the while she'd been dancing her troubles away!

She shuddered, her mouth resisting his for a second.

Then she opened for him. Soft. Warm. Drugging in the extreme. His hands trailed over her hips to cup her behind, the pliant leather almost non-existent as he moulded her to him. With a soft moan, she twined her arms around his neck, her shapely body plastering itself against his.

Dios, but she incensed his every cell. He'd returned with a plan, a strictly professional one he'd intended to present to her. Seeing her with O'Hare, their heads close together, on the verge of *dirty dancing*, had firmly altered the landscape of his clearly nonsensical misgivings.

Far from the distraught creature he'd thought he'd encounter on his return, he'd been confronted with a sensual being intent on driving every red-blooded male in the nightclub into a sexual frenzy.

Spreading her wings...

Clearly he'd imagined her earlier distress.

She moved against him, sleek and sinuous. His blood pounded thicker, his heart pistoning hard against his ribs. Javier widened his stance, pinned her against the wall and brought one hand between them.

Lifting the hem of her top, he dragged his nails across her abdomen. It was the lightest of touches and yet she shivered as if caught in an arctic storm.

Her responsiveness hadn't lessened in the time since they were last together. The gratifying thought spurred him on. A quick, deft fumble, a lowering of her zipper, and his fingers were sliding over her silky skin, beneath lace made hot by her arousal.

Her shocked gasp singed his mouth as he found his mark. His free hand clasped her nape, and he broke the kiss. 'Is this what you want, Principessa? Is this the type of *fun* you're looking for?' He thrummed the wet, nerve-engorged bud. Her tiny scream barely echoed through the alley, the greedy roll of her hips already seeking more.

He gave her a little more, grimly gratified when her fingers bit into his neck. 'Javier! *Dio mio...per favore...*'

He drew back a touch, stared down at her enraptured face and knew he had to have her. All logical reasons why not be damned. 'You'll get your chance to spread your wings. But you do it with me. And only me. *Comprende?*'

Eyes clamped shut as she chased her elusive pleasure, she whispered, *'Tu sei pazzo!'*

'I'm far from crazy. Since you're so keen to embrace a whole new you, go right ahead. But if you think I'm going to sit back and watch you throw yourself at every idiot who smiles at you, think again. Consider our contract renegotiated. From now on, *I* will be the one to give you pleasure.'

Her head dropped against the wall, her breath coming in aggrieved pants. *'Santa Maria,* I'm *not* having this conversation right now.'

He teased her saturated opening, earning a frustrated whimper.

'Open your eyes, *querida*,' he commanded silkily. 'Closing your eyes and wishing your troubles away only work in fairy tales.'

Eyes heavy with arousal, frustration, and eternally enthralling, met his. Keeping their gazes locked, he leaned forward and licked her lower lip. He nipped at the soft flesh, then pressed one finger inside her. 'Mine. You will be mine, *exclusively*, until I say otherwise,' he breathed.

Another shudder rippled through her, followed by several more as he increased the friction. He drew back again, his senses leaping with the need to witness her surrender.

'*Per favore*…please,' she groaned, her head falling forward onto his shoulder.

He slid his finger deep into her tight, silky heat, then growled as she found her release seconds later.

A horn sounded nearby, followed by shouts of revelry tearing through the night air. Javier wondered dazedly how he'd kept upright as the sweet sounds of her climax echoed for his ears alone.

One minute passed, then two. Stepping back, he righted her clothes.

'Can you walk?' he demanded thickly.

Another tiny shudder, then she nodded. '*Sì.*'

He pressed a kiss to her temple, then slung his arm over her shoulders, gratified when she burrowed into him.

His limo idled on the kerb, the back door guarded by Antonio. Javier helped her into it, and shut the door behind them. When she went to move away, he stayed her. She collapsed against him, but remained silent as the car crawled through traffic. Although her breathing steadied, he knew she hadn't fallen asleep from the furtive glances she cast at him.

'We can discuss this now, or we can discuss it in the morning. Either way, my conditions remain the same.'

She pulled away, and this time he let her have a little distance. She would be back where she belonged soon, anyway.

'Why?' she queried.

'Why what?'

'Why do you want me?'

A bitter laugh scraped his throat. 'If I could explain the mysteries of sexual chemistry, I would be a far richer man.' He slid his fingers into her hair. 'But I want you. Badly. And you want me.'

'You can't hold me to a new, *sexual* contract. That's deplorable,' she disputed hotly, but he didn't miss her lingering glance at his mouth, and the unsteady breath she took when her eyes met his.

She wanted him. Almost as badly as he wanted her, despite having come apart in his arms mere minutes ago.

The memory lit fresh flames in his groin.

'No, but I did talk to your father again. He believes you are on the verge of reaching a new agreement with me. So let's hear it.'

Alarm chased over her face, followed by a touch of uncertainty. A swallow moved her throat. 'I was going to ask for an amendment to our agreement.'

'One that benefits your father?'

'One that buys me a little time. An early release of the second quarter payment to him and a percentage of my future earnings will end our business relationship. And I get to find out what happened with my mother.'

Javier allowed the wave of sympathy that surged at her words. He'd been caught between a rock and a hard place where his mother was concerned. Having no immediate solution to the problem of his father wasn't an issue he'd relished. But *that* would all be over soon. He scoured her face, took in the change. An instant later the memory of another man's hands on her eroded his sympathy.

'You can have your amendment tomorrow. If you give me what I want.' Still holding her captive, he traced his finger over her passion-bruised bottom lip, the urge to kiss her again firing up inside him. 'And before you revert to the tired line of not wanting me, remember that I could've taken you in that alley, completely and as many times as I wanted, and you would've begged me for more. This way we put our cards on the table. There will be no illusions or misapprehension on either of our parts. And you can't get on your high horse afterwards and claim you weren't thinking straight.'

Perfect eyelashes swept down. 'And if I don't agree?'

'Your father pursues his imprudent financial schemes until such time as the fallout adversely affects me and my company. Then I take steps to hold you both accountable and you lose what little assets you have.'

She opened her mouth to speak as the car stopped in front of his penthouse building.

He stopped her by pressing his lips against hers, hot and hard, then pulled away before temptation got out of hand. 'Take the night, think about it and give me your answer in the morning. I know you'll choose wisely.'

'You're so certain you know what I'll decide?'

He shrugged. 'Besides the pleasure you'll receive in my bed, there's the added benefit that once your father knows you're mine, truly mine, he'll think twice about threatening you again.'

'So those are my two choices? Choose you or choose him?'

'The writing's been on the wall for a while, Principessa. This way you know you're backing the right horse.'

He flung the door open and grabbed her hand. In the bright light of the foyer, he caught a clearer glimpse of her outfit and cursed himself for giving her the night to agree to his demands. The ache in his groin alone threatened to fracture his mind.

Although his every instinct screamed at him to go after her when she muttered goodnight and made a beeline for her bedroom, Javier stayed put.

Morning would come soon enough.

Carla Nardozzi would be his.

She would most certainly *not* be his.

Not in the cold, calculated way he'd spelt out in the darkness of his car. There had to be another way. She toyed with getting Draco to negotiate on her behalf, but her agent had done his part. This renegotiation of the contract was private, between her and Javier. Besides, based on the current strained relationship between the two men, she didn't think

Javier would welcome her turning to the man he thought she was trying to make jealous three years ago.

She tossed in the pre-dawn light and a different dilemma flared again. The shameful knowledge that Javier had been right, that she would've given herself to him in that alley, couldn't be erased. The release she'd received at his hand had been gratifying, but it'd barely dented the depth of her hunger. She could continue to deny it, continue to keep him at arm's length with her words alone. But they would be lies.

That didn't mean she had to give in.

The bed linen twisted around her heated body as she fidgeted. The simple truth was, had their circumstances been different, had they been meeting again after three years as casual acquaintances reconnecting again, Carla knew she would've given in to her body's clamouring. The pull between them would've been too great to deny herself a chance to explore it. Especially having already experienced the intensity of it.

But all that aside, she knew there was no way she could walk away from the chance to find out what happened to her mother, the opportunity to finally lay her ghost to rest. Hadn't she only yesterday vowed to do everything she could to get to the truth?

Just as Javier had brought himself to do the unthinkable and tolerate the father who'd rejected him at every turn all his life, for the sake of his mother, didn't she owe her mother the same? Was the body she'd already given willingly to Javier, and couldn't deny she would give again were their circumstances different, suddenly too high a price to pay?

She didn't deny the irony of finding common ground with the very man who was threatening that ground, but as the sun crested the horizon Carla rubbed her eyes and faced the decision head-on.

In a few short hours, she would agree to become Javier Santino's mistress.

Exactly why that sent a terrible little thrill through her, she shut her eyes firmly against examining.

'Ah, there you are. *Buenos días*, Carla. I was beginning to think I would be subjected to a lonely breakfast by myself.'

Carla refrained from pointing out the many breakfasts she'd had on her own since arriving in New York. Nor did she imagine for an instant that Javier's easy tone was in any way a barometer for his mood. What really spelled out his mood were the narrowed, piercing eyes that tracked her from the dining-room door to her seat. Silently, she accepted as she sat down that she might have contributed to that look by oversleeping past her usual first light waking.

With indolent grace, he scoured her face, now devoid of last night's make-up, before leaning forward to tuck a strand of her hair behind her ear. The action, so poignantly gentle, and yet so ruthlessly calculated, sent a tremor through her.

'Javier, I've come to a decision,' she started, wanting to get this over and done with as quickly as humanly possible.

'Let us eat first, *chiquita*. That way neither of us risks a spoilt appetite if the news delivered and whatever reaction it produces isn't agreeable to our digestive systems.'

He nodded to Felipe, who hovered discreetly nearby. Sterling silver domed dishes were unveiled and her plate heaped with all her favourite foods. Managing a stiff smile at the butler, she attempted to make a dent in the poached egg, toast and slices of ham before her. Fresh fruit appeared on another platter. Before she could shake her head, Javier picked up a large chunk of pineapple and sliced it into smaller pieces.

Forking a square, he presented it to her. His eyes were still narrowed, gauging her stance on a subject he suddenly seemed reluctant to discuss.

For a moment, Carla wondered if he was nervous about her decision. Although it seemed impossible to imagine it now, she'd witnessed his pain and misery when he'd talked about his childhood. His vulnerability had shown then, and she wondered if it was there now, hidden beneath his brusque and intense demeanour.

She took the offered fruit and watched him feed himself a piece. In silence, he shared the pineapple between them until it was finished. Then he sat back and finished his coffee.

When she set her own empty cup down he rose. 'Now we've had our fill, let's talk.'

He walked out of the dining room, the white shirtsleeves rolled up his forearms and the dark grey trousers lending him a casual air she knew was false. Thinking they would conduct their business in the taciturn surroundings of his study, she was taken aback when he led her out onto the vast, wraparound terrace. Sunlight framed his lithe form, bathing his hair and body in a vibrant glow as he strolled over to the high terrace wall, and observed the iconic view for a full minute before he faced her.

'Tell me your decision,' he said abruptly.

Carla started to lace her fingers, then grimaced when her cast got in the way. She walked forward, stopping several feet away when the immutable force of his aura threatened to swallow her whole. 'I agree to your conditions.' Clearing her throat so her voice emerged stronger, she continued, 'I'll be your...whatever term you want to place on this association of ours.'

His eyes turned dark and stormy. 'The term is *mine*, *querida*. You'll be mine.'

Her breath shuddered out. '*Sì*. I'll be yours,' she whispered.

She wasn't sure what she expected. A triumphant fist pump? A battle cry of victory? No, those weren't quite Javier's style.

'Come here, Carla,' he commanded after a full minute of stomach-churning silence, his voice steeped in quiet authority.

She went. She was long past the point of equivocating

and had accepted that this would be her fate. At least for the short term.

Strong, corded arms banded her waist, bringing her flush against his hard, hot male body. From chest to knees, she was plastered against him, barely able to breathe for the strength and power of him, for the electricity zapping crazily through her body. Breath growing shallower by the second, Carla waited to be swept off her feet. For what had started in the dark, smoky alley last night to progress to its turbulent conclusion.

And yet, now she was in his arms, Javier didn't seem in a hurry to speak, to take what belonged to him. One hand left her waist and trailed upward, the single tie securing her hair pulled away and disposed of before he slid his fingers through the strands to cradle the back of her head. The massage was as unexpected as it was alarmingly soothing. And even more disconcerting were the feelings that surfaced when he tucked her head into his chest, his chin lightly resting on her crown.

Safe and secure.

Both emotions absurd, of course, considering she was fully aware of why he'd demanded this sacrifice from her. The evidence of it was a hot and rigid presence against her belly, a reminder that whatever was going to happen between them would be purely physical.

But Carla stood still, allowed herself to breathe in his scent, let his arms draw her even closer into his body, and, just for the hell of it, brought her arms to rest against his chest.

'Eres mio,' he murmured throatily after an eternity.

Although she didn't understand the words, there was a profound sense of claiming within them, and for a single instant Carla let herself wonder...*what if...?* The judder through her heart warned her she was risking being badly burnt by fire; warned her to end this bizarre lull.

Javier beat her to it.

Releasing her, he took a casual step back and extracted his phone. 'My lawyers will have the financial amendments to the contract drawn up and delivered for you to sign by lunchtime. Felipe will witness it,' he stated matter-of-factly. 'I'm assuming you don't want the usual cooling-off period to apply?' He raised one eyebrow at her.

To counter the bereft feeling spiking through her, she crossed her arms. 'No, I don't. I believe in getting the inevitable over with.'

'I'll assume you're talking about your father, and not us. If you're referring to us, then please accept that there will be no *getting it over with* any time soon.'

Her insides jerked in alarm. 'Are you sure? Your attention span when it comes to your women hasn't changed, has it? So if I'm lucky, I'll only need to amuse you for two weeks, maybe three at the most?'

He sauntered towards her, his fingers tapping out numbers on the flat screen of his phone. He lifted it to his ear as he reached her, his free hand capturing her chin, his thumb conducting a lazy, fiery sweep over her bottom lip. 'I've waited three years to have you again, *dulce* Carla. If you think there will be a swift conclusion to what is about to happen between us, you have my advance sympathy.'

Before she could speak past the bolt of consternation that lanced her, he was turning away, speaking clear instructions into the phone. The buzzing in her ears prevented her from hearing what was being said, and, in a way, Carla was thankful. At some point in the night, she'd convinced herself this would be short-term thing, a way for Javier to satisfy his need for vengeance before he finally set her free. The idea that he didn't intend to do just that was scary enough, without listening to him spell out his full ownership of her to faceless lawyers over the phone.

She jumped when his hand arrived at her nape. A swathe of hair was pushed out of the way as his other arm reclaimed her waist, this time bringing her back to his front. His mouth found her heated skin, and trailed lazily over it, before drifting to her ear. 'I have to head to the office now. If you need any clarification on the contract, feel free to call me. Otherwise, Felipe has instructions to pack a suitcase for you. I'll see you at the airport tonight.'

She turned sharply, and his lips grazed the corner of her mouth. Before she lost the already fraying train of thought, she blurted, 'Airport? Where are we going?'

'We fly to Miami tonight.'

Miami. Where she'd first lost her head, and her innocence to him. 'I…why do I need to come along for a business trip?'

He tasted her with a light bite, then soothed the graze with his tongue. Carla couldn't help the desperate shiver that coursed through her.

'It's not a business trip, *amante*. I'm going to try that time-off thing again. First, to celebrate you returning to my bed. Then to celebrate my birthday in two weeks' time.'

CHAPTER TEN

JAVIER'S LUXURY BEACHFRONT property was just as resplendent and opulent as she remembered it. Set over three floors with a master suite poised on a mezzanine level above the top floor, the all-white mansion was ablaze with strategically placed floodlights as Javier guided her across the large expanse of green grass that separated the helipad from the residence.

The hand at her back stayed as they entered and were greeted by the six-strong staff. Carla tuned out as Javier conversed in rapid-fire Spanish with the buxom older woman who was his housekeeper. Instead, she looked around the interior, memories flooding her brain.

The huge main salon beyond wide double doors was where she'd seen Javier the moment she'd entered the house with Maria and Draco three years ago. It'd been almost as if he'd been waiting for her, his eyes had zeroed in on her instantly, and he'd never let up the intensity of his scrutiny and attention. Not for one moment.

Not until she'd been in his bed.

Then it'd increased a hundredfold.

'Taking a trip down memory lane on your own, *querida*? You don't think it rude not to wait for me before reliving the spectacular experience of our first coming together?'

She jumped at the mocking voice. Face flaming at the thought that he'd say such a thing in front of his staff, she turned away from the colonial Spanish-themed décor, away from the sweeping staircase where he'd nearly lost control and taken her that night. But the staff were nowhere in sight, having been dismissed while she'd been lost in her lustful recollections.

Meeting his bold gaze, she fought not to blush again. He

meant to torture her at every turn. But she was a step away from learning the truth about what happened to her mother. She had to hold that thought firm and true to see her through this. Even if the anticipation of what was going to happen here tonight rushed a continuous stream of almost debilitating excitement through her blood.

'I thought it would be rude to force you to relive something you obviously still find a touchy subject,' she countered.

His lips compressed. 'But I intend to replace those unfortunate memories with better ones.'

'Is that why you brought me here? To rewrite history?'

'Trying to rewrite history is impossible. But there's no reason why you shouldn't be allowed to make a better impression this time round.'

'Has anyone told you how impossibly arrogant you are?' she launched from the depths of the trepidation shaking through her.

'Has anyone told you how utterly delicious you are when you're trying to hide your anxiety with useless bravado?'

She flicked a dismissive hand. 'You're being ridiculous... again.'

He caught her hand, used it to pull her to him, then dragged her behind him to the breathtakingly beautiful salon. He paused in the middle of the gold-carpeted room and captured her jaw in his hands. 'And you're acting like a timid little virgin.' His face hardened. 'Drop the act, Carla,' he sliced at her. 'I'm choosing not to dwell on the other lovers you've had since you were last in my bed and what they would've wanted from you, but if you think that you playing some sort of sacrificial damsel turns me on, trust me, it doesn't.'

She barely managed to suppress a gasp, and tore her gaze from his.

'You know how crazy it makes me when you don't look at me when I'm talking to you, *querida*.'

She shook her head. '*Santa Maria*, can we please just get this over and done with?' she blazed at him, still studiously avoiding his gaze.

'We will not, as you say, get this over and done with. Constanza is preparing our dinner, which we will enjoy—'

'I'm not hungry,' she interjected. 'I had a late lunch.'

'Indeed you did, but I have it on good authority you barely touched the insubstantial sandwich you had Felipe prepare for you. So perhaps you want to come clean, and tell me what's really bothering you?'

She cast around for something to say, anything that would disguise her internal chaos. But the more she dwelled on what was to come, the more her senses unravelled.

She cast a swift glance at him, but the moment their eyes connected, she couldn't look away. Her breath shook out of her lungs as she blurted, 'I'm not... I don't...'

A look crossed his face, a flash of frightening bleakness before his expression settled back into its usual haunting, arrogant beauty. 'You don't...what? Want me?' he queried icily.

Saying yes she wanted him more than her next breath was dangerous. Saying no would be a lie. She hesitated, and with each second his expression grew tauter. Knowing she was only damning herself, she licked her lips. 'Javier...please—'

He swung her into his arms before she managed to form the right words. In quick, commanding strides, he crossed to the far side of the room. The lift tucked discreetly into the corner of the room blended effortlessly with the décor. A thumb print scan granted them access. Javier entered and the doors slid shut, sealing them inside.

Carla tried to wriggle free, but he held her tight, a warning growl emitting from his throat as the lift shot upward. She was still grappling with her words when it stopped and the doors slid open.

She hadn't forgotten the sheer magnificence of the master suite in Javier's mansion. But three years ago she'd been too intoxicated with his presence to take in the smaller details. This time she forced herself to look around, tried to find anything that would ground the runaway emotional freight train inside her. The retractable roof that displayed the spectacular skylight at night was still above her head, half opened to catch glimpses of a few bright stars set against a velvet backdrop. Unlike the priceless works of art that decorated his house, his bedroom only boasted four pieces. A bust of some god-like icon, two Renaissance paintings she knew without looking too closely were masterpieces, and, in the space between his bedroom and private living room, a white baby grand piano on top of which stood a simple wooden-framed picture.

Carla hadn't had the chance to get a closer look at the photo, but she thought it was of his mother.

She wasn't granted a chance now as he swung sharply towards the bed.

'You insist on denying what's between us when we both know it's a useless lie. You want me to force you to admit you want me, is that it? So that when you close your eyes to sleep you can pretend every whisper and moan was coerced from you?'

'No, Javier—'

'Well, think again.' His voice was soft and deadly. 'Before we're done tonight you will beg me to take you. And you will beg for it each time after that.'

She gasped as he caught the hem of her long-sleeved, cowl-neck dress and pulled it over her head. It landed at her feet without ceremony, leaving her in the platform heels and the matching peach bra and panty set she'd donned before they left New York.

The bite of hunger on his face was undeniable, but his mouth still twisted as he stared down at her. 'At least you didn't wear white. That would've taken things a step too far, *si*?'

She shivered at his raw, intense scrutiny, her nipples peaking with harsh demand as his gaze dropped and lingered at where the lace cupped her breasts. Heat lanced her, the ferocious fever roaring through her veins just from the look in his eyes.

With the grace of a magnificent predator, he circled her, eliciting decadent goosebumps on her flesh as he trailed sultry air over her with his movements. He stopped for an interminable age behind her, until every nerve in her body screamed for relief.

'Exquisite,' he rasped.

Finally, she felt him reach out and slowly untie her hair from its customary knot. The tresses fell heavily onto her shoulders. His fingers sank into them, much as they had this morning on his terrace in New York.

'I don't like your hair all caught up. I want it free to run my hands through whenever I feel like it. You will not wear it up again while we're here. Understood?' he rasped in her ear.

Another shudder rolled over her. Her throat clogged, she could barely answer. 'Yes.'

'Good.' Sliding his hands from her hair, he grasped her shoulders and turned her round. For an instant a naked, bewildered look was on his face, then it disappeared just as quickly. 'Kiss me, Carla,' he demanded.

Her heart faltered, then banged with renewed vigour against her ribs. Swallowing, she closed the gap between them, her heels lending her a fleeting confidence as she lifted herself the last few inches to press her lips against his. A snapped-off growl punched between them. Head swimming, she opened her lips and tasted him. Hot and virile, he was like a drug she couldn't stay away from. Feeling bolder, she deepened the kiss, her arms lifting to slide around his neck, then glided her tongue along his lower lip.

Firm hands grasped her waist, plastering her to him before his hands slid down to cup her pert behind. In a move that was shockingly erotic, he rolled her against his raging erection, the blatant intent behind the move arrowing need straight between her thighs. Unable to help herself, she pressed even closer.

A harsh exhalation burned her lips before he took over the kiss. Commanding, potently male, he devoured her mouth with ruthless vigour. Just when she didn't think she could stand the flames of desire, he picked her up and laid her on the bed.

Heart racing even faster, she watched, dazed as he ripped his buttons free and tugged off his shirt. Dry-mouthed, Carla stared at the sleek beauty of him. Smooth and toned without a spare ounce of flesh, Javier was truly breathtaking. Her awe at his amazing body tripled when he unbuckled his belt and kicked away his trousers and boxers.

Dio mio, he was impressive. Far more than she'd allowed herself to remember during those secret nights when she'd been unable to stem the memories. Her breath stalled as he prowled to the bed. Slowly, he tugged her shoes off, swiftly followed by her bra and panties. From the bedside drawer, he extracted a condom, which he tossed on the bed.

Then he wrapped his hands around her ankles and drew her legs apart. From head to toe she was exposed before him. And she was incapable of hiding. Her limbs were his to command as he pleased. He arranged her legs around him, then he bent his impressive body over her.

He kissed the silken space between her breasts, taking his time to cup each mound, mould her flesh in his big hands and roll her turgid nipples between his fingers.

Her back arched off the bed as sensation snaked through her like a live wire. Each moan was answered with a deeper caress, a harder nip until her head was thrashing on the pillow. Catching one nipple in his mouth, he rolled the tight peak over his tongue before he sucked deep.

'Ah, *Dio*,' she gasped as harsher sensations arrowed between her legs.

She was burning up. Every caress drew her closer to the

peak she'd only experienced at this man's hands. Her hips twisted, need wild and untamed clamouring through her. His lips finally left her breasts, trailing lower down her body, bestowing hotter, more fervent kisses over her skin.

He reached the juncture of her thighs and she stopped breathing. Intent fierce and clear on his face, he lowered his head. At the first bold kiss, her eyes rolled shut.

He pulled away and froze.

'Eyes open, Carla. Tell me you want this. There will be no more hiding,' he instructed hoarsely. 'No more pretending this isn't happening.'

She forced herself to stare into his molten gaze and not drown in the torrential storm raging over her senses. 'I want this. Please…'

His nails raked lightly over her lower belly. Then again, harder. Pleasure like never before exploded beneath her skin. 'Again,' he demanded fiercely.

'I want you, Javier,' she murmured his name, needing to ground herself. Another drag of his nails.

With a deep groan, he rolled his tongue over her, expertly finding that most sensitive bud that sent her wild. His exploration was brazen, his determination to wring every ounce of response from her a purpose that raged from his every pore. From one heartbeat to the next, she was cresting that blissful peak, her senses in free fall as ecstasy slammed into her.

The sound of foil ripping was the precursor to the deeper, longer, more decadent pleasure she knew awaited her when she surfaced from the depths of her blinding release.

Javier reared over her, taking hold of her injured hand to rest it on the pillow above her head. Then he planted himself between her thighs, his full weight supported on his elbows as he stared down at her.

'Who do you belong to?'

'You. I'm yours. Please,' she gasped.

A hard, possessive kiss on her lips, followed by a deep

exploration with his tongue, then he surged into her with one deep, true thrust.

The pace was steady, his gaze fierce on her face as he took complete possession of her. Carla wanted to look away, suddenly afraid of what he would see in her eyes, especially since she wasn't sure what her raw emotions betrayed. But the dark depths of his gaze held her prisoner, each gleam mesmerising, his open hunger almost as absorbing as what his body was doing to hers. Uncontrollable shudders rolled through her as pressure mounted. Her moans mingled with his deep groans until they melded into one erotic litany that swirled around them.

'Carla,' he whispered her name as he plunged his fingers into her hair and ramped up the tempo of his thrusts.

The sound of her name on his lips, like this, shattered something inside her. As much as she wanted to convince herself this was an emotionless coupling, she knew it wasn't.

Not when she was floating out of herself, her heart unfurling like a flower towards the sun.

A touch of panic seized her. 'Javier, *non posso...* I... please...'

Javier felt a deep shudder reel through him, the last vestiges of doubt washing away beneath the pleasure overtaking him. He'd pondered whether he'd done the right thing by acting this way, by bringing her here, to the place where she'd scored a direct hit to his pride. Right in the moment, he knew nothing could persuade him otherwise. She was exactly where he wanted her to be, in his bed, beneath him, his name on her lips and ecstasy stamped in her gorgeous eyes. He trailed a hand down her side, felt her very skin strain towards him, and he wanted to roar his triumph.

For far too long, he'd wanted her. Had wondered whether he'd dreamed their potent chemistry and was savagely delighted that he hadn't.

She made another fractured sound, a twist between a sob and a moan. *That* singular sound that spelled how close she was imploded every useless thought. Her hips twisted up to meet his, her slick channel a hot fist around his manhood.

The roar that punched from him was as alien as the peak he crested a minute later. Both far surpassed the norm and threw him headlong into a kaleidoscopic unknown. Breathing ragged and desperate, he buried his face in her neck and deliberately emptied his mind of thought.

He couldn't deal with the unknown at the moment. Hell, he felt as if he were skating the very edge of sound reasoning from the moment he'd taken her call yesterday afternoon. Among those absurd feelings, the need to cherish and protect were ones he couldn't comprehend. He had no intention of comprehending them. At long last, she was back in his bed. That would be the extent of his personal dealings with Carla.

He raised himself up and stared down into her face. Lust-glazed eyes met his and he exhaled when they didn't immediately slide away. Leaning down, he tasted her kiss-swollen lips, groaning when they clung briefly to his. He indulged them both for a minute, before reluctantly pulling away to dispose of the condom.

On his return he saw that she had rolled onto her side, away from him. Javier tried not to let the sight disturb him. She would not be going far this time. Nor would any attempt to reject him ring true. Her responses had been genuine. And borderline innocent, just like the first time. Almost as though she hadn't taken any other lover since him.

He frowned. The urge to probe the extent of her sexual history hovered on his tongue, but he curbed it. Simply because that didn't matter in the here and now. And not because the idea that she might have been with someone else messed with his head.

Sliding into bed, he gathered her close, releasing a trapped breath when she came willingly, melted against him. She laid her injured hand on his chest and he found himself reaching for it, smoothing a kiss over the cast before curling his fingers over it.

She raised her head and her eyes met his. The quiet fire he'd missed seeing in them was back. But so was the bewildering feeling powering through his own body. Leaning down, he kissed her one more time. When her lids drooped, he settled her firmly against his body.

'Sleep now, if you want to, *querida*. You've passed the first test with flying colours.'

He tried not to read too much into her response when she murmured, 'I'm so glad,' then promptly drifted off to sleep. But he was wide awake several hours later, staring up at the stars, his mind abuzz with unsettling thoughts. When one thought kept recurring—that he was dreading the approach of morning in case history repeated itself with a vengeance—he grunted and kicked away the tangled sheets, a wicked thread of satisfaction spiking through him when Carla opened her eyes. He was donning protection and sliding into her before she was fully awake. After that, he encouraged her to join him in raiding the fridge.

Then, sated, he dragged her back to bed.

Carla awoke splayed out on top of Javier. She knew he was awake because his fingers teased through her hair in long, lazy movements. Her heart kicked hard as the events of last night flooded her mind. But as much as the euphoria made itself felt, it was the bright sunlight filtering in through the curtains that made her stomach dip in alarm.

Her last experience of the morning after had been abysmal. And she didn't doubt that the memory would be in the forefront of Javier's mind too.

'I'm willing to forget our previous experience if you are.'

Her head jerked up. Polished mahogany flecked with gold regarded her steadily, but she saw the steady tic in his cheek as his fingers continued to play with her hair.

With every cell in her body, she wanted to say yes, to brush the unfortunate incident under the carpet and forget it'd ever happened. But she owed him an explanation. 'No, I don't want to forget it. I want to explain.'

His eyes darkened but he nodded. 'Very well. Go on.'

She bit her lip. 'That week we met was the first time I'd ever been given any form of freedom or time off since I was twelve years old. The day I was accepted into the international figure-skating programme, my life stopped being my own.'

Javier frowned. 'I thought you loved it.'

'I did. I do,' she replied, but Carla knew the ambivalence she'd been feeling lately bled into her voice. 'It's the only thing I excel at, but it's hard to love something when you know without it you're nothing.'

His frown deepened. 'Nothing? What are you talking about?'

'If I wasn't a figure skater what would I be?'

'Whatever you want to be. You're the only one who can set limitations on yourself.'

She shook her head. 'That's just it. I don't want to be anything else, but I was never given a choice of what I *could* be. Does that make sense?'

His fingers trapped in her hair. '*Sí*, it makes sense. But I don't understand what this has to do with what happened three years ago.'

A flicker of shame singed her. 'My father was against me coming to New York with Maria and Draco. He wanted me to return to Tuscany with him for the two-week break, like always. We…fought badly, but I refused to back down. But every minute I was away I was terrified of what he'd do.'

'What do you mean? Did he physically hurt you?'

'No, but he…had his ways when I disobeyed him.'

Javier flipped their positions and reared over her. 'What ways?'

'He would have my trainer double my training, or my favourite horse would suddenly be lent to a neighbour's daughter for the summer.'

His jaw tightened. 'He wanted to show you he was in control.'

'*Sì*. But three years ago, I turned twenty-one. And I challenged his authority by taking my two-week break without him. But that wasn't all I did. I called my mother and begged her to intercede with him on my behalf over his controlling behaviour.' Her voice broke, the emotions she'd held in check for so long bubbling to the surface.

A firm hand cupped her jaw, his thumb trailing over her cheek. 'What did he do?'

'He called me...during your party. He told me he was disappointed in me. That I shouldn't have got my mother involved in our lives again.'

'Again?' he queried.

Carla swallowed. 'She left when I was ten. I won the regional skating championship when I was nine, and had been scouted for the nationals. My mother thought I was too young for the intensity of the training. My father disagreed. They fought for a solid year and, towards the end, their arguments got more intense. My father never physically abused her, but I could tell he was close to it.' She shuddered in remembrance of the latent violence that had lingered in those confrontations. 'The week before she left, she cried every night. When she told me she was leaving, I was shattered, but I was also relieved.'

Javier's eyes darkened with quiet fury. 'She never contemplated taking you with her?'

'My father would never have allowed her to do that. He worked in a factory when I was a child. The moment he realised my potential, he gave up his job. I was his ticket to a dream life and he wasn't about to let it go.' Bitterness and sorrow duelled for supremacy within her. Javier saw it, leaned down and placed a gentle kiss on her lips.

Tears prickled her eyes but she blinked them away.

'So you reached out to her when you turned twenty-one...?'

'My father had planned out my life for the next five years, and I was suffocating.'

'You could've walked away, started afresh with a new management team.'

She shook her head. 'We're locked into a management agreement that ends when I'm twenty-five. Or at least we were. Once this new deal goes through, I'll be free of him.'

He swore under his breath. 'So your mother was your only option?'

Her heart shuddered, regret biting deep. 'She agreed to talk to him. She was on her way to Tuscany when I came to Miami. He called me during your party, and I'd never heard him so angry. Something in his voice scared me, but I convinced myself it was nothing.'

'That's why you got drunk?'

She gave a shaky nod. 'I wanted to drown him out... to drown everything out.' She risked a glance at him and found his steady, intense gaze on her. 'I didn't regret what happened to us, but...'

'But?' he bit out.

'But, I would've done things differently if I'd had another chance.'

'How differently?'

'I would've started the evening sober, for a start.'

'*Sí*, but you weren't drunk by the end of it.'

Unable to resist, she grazed her fingers over his morning stubble. 'That's because *you* made sure I wasn't. Can you imagine if it'd been someone else less honourable than you?'

He tensed. 'Did we agree not to mention other people while you're in my bed?'

'I didn't mean...that was a hypothetical question, Javier,' she admonished.

He gave a stiff, arrogant shrug. 'Spare yourself my hypothetical wrath and stick to your story, *querida*,' he suggested.

'I woke up the next morning hating myself for hiding behind my mother and not facing my father. I hated the circumstances that brought us together and I didn't handle it well.'

'So you deliberately let me believe you were going from my bed to Angelis's?'

Heat crawled up her face. *'Mi dispiace molto.'*

'And the dates in London? The kiss in Tuscany?'

'All completely platonic. I'm not in love with Draco, Javier. I swear. I never have been.'

He stared at her in silence for a full minute, before he nodded. *'Bene,'* he replied gruffly, then took her mouth in another heart-stopping kiss.

After several minutes, he raised his head. 'We seem to have come full circle, Carla. Give me your word that you're mine and I'll let this matter rest.'

'I'm yours,' she affirmed.

He kissed her again, then nodded for her to continue.

'For years I'd been promising myself that when I could I would walk away from my father. But in the end I wanted everything. My career, my father, my mother, everything in harmony. A stupid wish, of course.'

His mouth twisted. 'The day we stop dreaming and striving for the unachievable is the day we die. Don't beat yourself up about it.'

'But don't you see? I wanted too much. Because she died.'

He stiffened. 'But you said you don't know how she died. How do you know it's because of what you asked of her?'

The thorns that had never quite melted away from her heart pierced her unbearably. 'Because if I hadn't got her involved she would still be alive. I begged her to intercede with my father, and she died because of it.'

CHAPTER ELEVEN

JAVIER SLOWLY PULLED back from her. The absence of his warmth struck her almost as deeply as the pain ravaging her insides. He sat with his back against the massive headboard, his features inscrutable. In the next instant, he pulled her up against him, one strong arm around her shoulders as he leaned her back against him.

'You believe your father did something to her or you wouldn't be torturing yourself this way,' he stated, cutting right to the heart of the matter.

Her breath caught. 'I don't want to think that…but I can't help myself.'

'Tell me what you know.'

'Not much. All I know is she went to Tuscany to talk to him. She didn't leave there alive. I found out she was dead a week after I left you, after I'd completed my three-day competition in Switzerland.'

'*Dios mio.* He didn't tell you?'

'He didn't want the news to affect my performance. The first I knew of her death was on the way to the funeral home. He said it was an accident, that he was sorry, but I needed to put it behind me as soon as possible.'

Carla didn't realise she was crying until his thumb brushed the moisture from her cheeks. Then, as if the flood-gates of her grief had been ripped open, thick sobs exploded from her heart. Javier held her closer, both arms folding her into his body as she purged her grief. Selfishly, she clung to him, knowing deep down that it was unwise, but unable to stop herself from soaking up his support.

Gentle words spoken in Spanish floated over her. Long moments later, her hiccups the only sound in the room, Carla attempted to pull away.

He held her still. 'Stay.'

'No, I shouldn't—'

'Reliving the past was bound to resurrect bad memories for you. Don't be distressed for needing a shoulder to lean on sometimes. We both know you're strong when you need to be.'

Her laughter was harsh and one hundred per cent self-deprecating. This time when she pulled away, he let her. Rising on her knees, she brushed away the last of her tears and faced him. 'Strong? If I was I wouldn't have left it another three years after her death to finally seek answers. I wouldn't be giving in to my father's demands for a *bribe* just so I find out how my own mother died. That doesn't make me strong!'

A muscle ticced in his jaw. 'We try to find answers the best way we can.'

She spiked her fingers through her hair, bewilderment raging high. 'I don't know why you're trying to make me feel better, Javier. If it hadn't been for me, your mother would be resting in peace by now.'

One corner of his mouth lifted in a grim smile. 'That was your father's doing, not yours. I was hacked off when I lumped you in with him. You can't be held accountable for his failures. For my part, trying to afford my mother some peace now doesn't alter the fact that I left her with Fernando for years, distanced myself as far away as I could.'

'You left because you wanted to make a better life for both of you,' she countered.

'*Sí*, but also because a part of me was disappointed that she wanted so very little for herself. That she was too weak to break away from his poisonous presence. No matter where she was in the world, she pined for him. It was a weakness I didn't understand. So in the end, I left her to it. And she died alone.'

Tears she'd thought were long spent clogged her throat

again. 'So you're saying we deserve this anguish we're both going through?'

A heavy shrug. 'We can accept our part in the theatre of our lives, even flog ourselves daily for it. But you can't lose yourself because of it.' His smile turned grimmer. 'Or let those rightly responsible get away with it.'

A cold shiver went through her. She might have fooled herself into believing she'd found common ground with Javier. That the shoulder he'd lent her had come without strings. As she watched him reach for her, she knew how wrong she'd been.

He might understand her plight, might even empathise on some level, but he still held her responsible for a large degree of his unresolved issues with his father.

And for that, she would continue to pay with her body.

Heart slamming hard in her lungs, and desperate not to let him see how his final words had affected her, she slid her arms around his neck as he rose from the bed and headed to the large, marble-floored bathroom.

'So…what now?'

'We take a shower and then I take you for an early lunch.'

Javier couldn't get to the bottom of his fury long enough to gain proper control of it. Hell, he could barely see past the red haze that crossed his vision each time he thought of what Olivio Nardozzi had, and continued to, put his daughter through.

He'd made love to Carla in the shower with an edge of rage he knew she'd felt. She'd been with him every step of the way, but he'd glimpsed the shaken look in her eyes afterwards as they'd dressed.

He'd known the other man was as self-centred and avaricious as they came, perhaps even more so than his own father—which was saying something—but he'd never imagined Olivio would put his own child through such raw turmoil.

As he navigated his sports car along the highway towards South Beach, he suppressed a crude curse. He'd spent the night mostly awake and had hated himself for it because he'd dreaded the morning would bring a repeat of Carla's rejection three years ago. What he hadn't expected was a wild swing in the opposite direction, a dropping of her guard and a complete baring of her soul that had left a previously unknown part of him touched and reeling. A part he didn't want to examine, much as he didn't want to examine the real reason he'd instigated this whole thing with Carla in the first place.

He glanced over at her, satisfaction pulsing through him that the subject of her and Angelis had finally been put to rest. Truth be told, now jealousy was no longer blinding him, he could see that Angelis had only ever been looking out for her. And three years ago, Carla hadn't actually come right out and confessed that she was in love with her agent, had she? Looking back, he realised it was the deeper effect of her father's actions that had fuelled his need for vengeance.

And even that need was dissipating.

She returned his gaze and he lost his train of thought as his eyes drifted over her.

Her stretchy cream dress ended a good few inches above her thighs, showing off her slim legs in a mouth-watering expanse of light golden flesh. The material skimmed her curves in a way that made his palms itch to follow each thread of cotton, and Javier was ridiculously jealous of the seat belt that rested between her breasts. As he watched, she twitched beneath his scrutiny, her hand lifting to tuck back the hair shifting in the breeze of his open-top car.

A different sort of turbulence attacked him, this time much lower in his body but equally insistent. And equally unsettling. Carla hadn't been far off in her accusation that his sexual liaisons were fleeting at worst and a step above short term at best. He certainly didn't crave any woman he dated after having her as many times as he'd had Carla in the last twelve hours. Yet, his body's continual reaction to her threatened to reduce him to hormonal teenager status.

'Are you going to spend the entire journey in silence?' she asked, her voice a touch shaky, he knew, from the thick, aggressive vibes he was throwing out.

He opened his mouth to respond in a way that would ease her agitation—another first for him—but then his gaze touched on her bound wrist. 'Your lawyers have been in touch about Blackwell's trial?' It wasn't really a question that required an answer. He'd kept up to date on what was happening with the ex-trainer in Italy.

She nodded. 'It's happening in three weeks. Draco says I don't need to be there. The video testimony is enough.'

He squashed the residual jealousy that lingered at the mention of her agent. 'When did you speak to him?'

'Yesterday.' A bold but wary glance flicked his way, her green eyes turning a shade darker. 'Javier?'

'Sí?' he responded, more than a little perturbed at how much pleasure his name on her lips brought him.

'You two used to be good friends, yes?'

His jaw tightened. 'What's your point?'

'You know what my point is.'

He shrugged. 'And I'm trying to be the bigger man here, but you kissed him at your charity event, did you not?'

She gasped. 'Surely you can't still be jealous about that? He's crazy about his fiancée!'

Javier's hands tightened on the steering wheel as he wondered why he couldn't get control of yet another irrational emotion. 'You can assess for yourself how I feel when we see Angelis at my party.'

Her eyes widened with surprise, then a touch of pleasure that made him grit his teeth. 'They're coming here?'

'Should I be put out that you've already forgotten about my birthday celebration?'

'I didn't think… I thought it would be just us.'

He captured her hand and brought it to his lips, his pulse

spiking at the touch of her silky skin. 'As much as I want to keep you all to myself, I need to uphold my *party hard* reputation. Angelis and his fiancée have already accepted my invitation. You want us to be friends again, make me forget that kiss and I'll give it a shot,' he half teased. 'You see? I can be progressive after all.'

Despite his words, Carla sensed his tension as they pulled up in front of a silver, futuristic-looking building opposite an inner city park. After helping her out, he handed his keys to a hovering valet and pulled her to his side.

A quick kiss at her temple turned into a trailing caress that ended at the corner of her mouth. Carla's pulse was dancing wildly by the time he straightened.

'Forgive me for the quick pit stop. I won't be long.'

Carla looked around the foyer with interest. Young executives buzzed around, their casual yet frenetic appearance indicating a creative atmosphere. 'What is this place?' she asked.

'My production design crew are based here. They have the altered specs for the tequila bottle ready for me to inspect.'

'I thought the design was finalised.'

A quizzical smile teased his sensual mouth. 'As did I. But inspiration struck and I went with it.'

Intrigued and more than a little surprised that he would bring her to inspect what was obviously a special project for him, Carla followed him into the lift. He positioned her in front of him, then proceeded to plant hot, shockingly erotic kisses on her neck.

When the lift pinged to a stop, he groaned. 'Perhaps I should've postponed this meeting. The timing of this wasn't the best idea.'

'Perhaps you should have,' she teased. 'Although I doubt it would've happened.'

He turned her around in his arms, his eyes narrowed as he scrutinised her face. 'You trying to make a point, *querida*?'

She shrugged, her heart doing a funny little dance at the predatory light in his eyes as his gaze dropped to her mouth. 'You keep threatening to take a day off, but I've yet to see you actually take one.'

The hands gripping her waist tightened a fraction before he set her free. 'I need intense stimulation otherwise I get bored. You think you're up to the task of providing me with such stimulation?' he rasped.

Heat flowed up her neck and completely engulfed her cheeks. 'There's only one way to find out...*caro*,' she countered bravely, unwilling to let on just how out of her element she really felt.

Dark, mesmeric eyes glinted with a feral light that strangled her breath. The hand that curled around hers was implacable, possessive. The urgent strides that had her trotting to keep up announced that her gauntlet had been accepted.

Carla was reeling from just what she'd let herself in for when Javier led them through double glass doors into a large room. The circular seating area contained an inner carpeted area with a raised platform. In the middle of it stood a tall object draped with black silk.

Three executives rose as they entered. All young, all eager to make an impression as they greeted Javier.

'Mr Santino. It's good to see you again.' The closest man shook hands with him.

Javier nodded to the other two, and, without letting go of her hand, walked to the middle of the room. 'I need to be elsewhere, gentlemen. I'd appreciate us getting on with it?' The statement was couched as a question, but the order was clear.

'Of course. The specs are just what you asked for.' The oldest in the group, clearly their leader, pulled back the silk cloth with a flourish.

What little oxygen remained in Carla's lungs after glimpsing the raw, predatory hunger in Javier's eyes evaporated as she stared at the redesigned tequila bottle. Much of the original design had remained the same, but where the neck had been a sleek line tapering to the rounded base, it now flowed in a distinct, unmistakably feminine shape. A shape that grew intimately familiar the more she stared at it.

Blushing to the roots of her hair, she tried to disentangle her fingers from Javier's. He held on tight, his eyes riveted to the life-size bottle as he rasped, 'Thank you for your hard work, gentlemen. Now if you'd be so kind as to leave us.'

The moment they were alone, she let out a stunned breath. 'You can't!'

He turned sizzling eyes to her. 'I can't what, *querida*?' he enquired silkily.

She gestured frantically at the bottle. 'You can't do…this.'

Circling behind her, he caught her around the waist and frogmarched her to the bottle. 'You belong to me. Give me one good reason why I cannot immortalise you however I wish to.'

She could think of one. *Dio*, she could think of several, the paramount of them being she only belonged to him on a temporary basis. None of what was happening between them would last beyond the next few weeks. But all her objections—and the peculiar pang that lanced her heart—vanished as she stared at the stunningly beautiful bottle.

His hands slipped from her waist, down to capture her hands. Linking her fingers with his, he brought them up to the neck of the bottle to grip the glass. Cool and smooth, the glass quickly warmed beneath her fingers. Or perhaps it was her imagination, and her fevered hormones alone were responsible for heating the bottle. He drew their hands down to rest on the upper curve, his head aligned with hers. She didn't need to turn her head to know he was staring at their joined hands on his creation.

'Now every time I touch this piece, I'll think of you,' he murmured in her ear.

Carla gave a single shake of her head, unable to comprehend the enormity of his testament. He might no longer hate her as much as she'd imagined he once did, but this…

She swallowed. 'Javier…'

'I wish I'd had this brought to the house. Now I need to get myself under control before we can leave.'

Another blush fired up her cheeks as she caught his meaning. She groaned as he pulled her back against him, the rigid line of his manhood searing into her behind for one charged moment before he set her free.

When she stumbled a few steps away, he didn't stop her. His gaze was once more on the bottle, his scrutiny blessedly clinical as he examined it fully. After a few minutes, he nodded with satisfaction and walked towards her.

The designers hovered outside and Javier invited them back in. Questions were fired out in rapid succession, most of which flew over her head as her gaze continually strayed to the bottle.

You belong to me…

The unyielding possession in those words should've frightened her, made her want to strike out for the independence she was desperately seeking in her life. But they reached into the heart of her, claiming a hitherto unknown part of her she hadn't realised was waiting for such a claiming. A claiming she was ready—

'Carla?'

She jumped. 'Yes?'

Javier smiled with the barest touch of mockery. 'It's time to go,' he intoned.

She blinked and realised the executives had left. Rising and casting one last glance at the bottle, she slipped a hand into the one he held out.

Javier led her out into the early afternoon sunshine. Thinking they were about to drive somewhere else, she followed him when he led her across the street and into the park.

'What are we doing here?'

'We're having lunch.'

Seeing no restaurant or anything resembling an impromptu picnic, she glanced back at him.

With a grin, he led her towards a food truck blaring out salsa music. The ruddy-faced chef greeted them in loud, rambling Spanish.

Javier responded, his graceful hand movements drawing her attention to his strong arms and the ripped body currently clothed in dark jeans and a sea-green rugby shirt. She watched him give an order she had no hope of following before leading her to the small table set for two at the side of the truck. Pulling out a chair for her, he went back to the truck and returned with two wrapped packages, paper plates, and two bottles of water.

She opened her package to a mouth-watering barrage of flavours. Aware that Javier was watching her, she took her first bite. And groaned.

'Dio mio.'

His grin widened. 'Very few things beat a well-prepared Cuban sandwich.' He passed her a bottle, then unwrapped his before taking a sizeable bite.

She took another bite. 'It's incredible.'

He nodded. 'It may be Cuban but it reminds me of a dish my mother used to prepare.' A slight frown wrinkled his brow, as if the memory was an unexpected one, but it was gone in a flash.

They'd delved far deeper into each other's histories than she knew he normally allowed. But she couldn't stop herself from probing deeper. 'Is that why you prefer to live here? Because it reminds you of home?'

His jaw clenched. 'I never had a home.'

'You know what I mean—'

He raised dark, intense eyes to her. 'Do I? I think we've got our lines crossed somewhere along the line. You had a home, albeit a brief one until your mother left. I had the equivalent of a prison, where each knock on the door either made my mother jump in fright or sick with inevitably thwarted anticipation. Neither of those two things made for anything resembling a *home*.'

'But despite all that, you had a parent who loved you. Does that not count for something?'

He chewed for a long time before he swallowed and pushed the remaining sandwich away. 'Not when you live in constant fear of being abandoned the moment the long-given promise showed signs of being fulfilled. And my father played his cards just so by keeping my mother from never giving up that her dreams would eventually come true. The end result being that I was always on tenterhooks that the only parent I had could be taken from me in the blink of an eye.'

She caught his hand in hers before she processed the action. 'I'm sorry.'

For a stark moment, he seemed perturbed by her sympathy. Then his lashes swept down. With a nod, he linked his fingers with hers, and grabbed his water bottle with his other hand. 'Finish your meal, *querida*. You have an afternoon of stimulating me to be getting on with.'

His low, deep laugh at her blush fired up her already scorching arousal. He didn't let up the sweltering possessive looks as he led her back to his car and slid behind the wheel. Nor did he make any bones about giving his staff the afternoon off once they returned home.

The moment the staff vacated the premises, he slid her dress over her head. Then he finally took her on the sweeping staircase, the way he'd threatened to three years ago.

The rest of the week continued in the same vein, with the exception of Javier working less and less each day. It was almost as if once he got into the rhythm of having time off, he threw himself into it with the same ruthless vigour he pursued every other area of his life. By the end of their first weekend, he'd introduced her to a high-speed trip on his latest speedboat—the JS1—a food tour of Little Havana, and sunbathing in the nude on his private beach. He'd swayed her through sensual salsa moves at an exclusive nightclub, which had abruptly ended when he'd dragged her off the dance floor and into his limo. They hadn't made it home and Carla had experienced her first, sizzling lovemaking session in the back of a car.

The only hiccup had arrived when Javier had proclaimed the nightclub to be the ideal venue for the tequila shoot and introduced her to his new, female, creative director. Her guarded query as to Darren's whereabouts had earned her a hard stare, followed by a terse, 'He's been promoted to head up a fascinating new project. In Alaska.'

Her wince hadn't gone unnoticed. Luckily, he'd let the moment pass.

By the middle of their second week, sensing his restlessness, Carla proposed a tentative start to the shoot. Jemma, the creative director, had hinted they could start with some strategic publicity shots that wouldn't show her cast.

They arrived at the nightclub just after lunch. The lights were dimmed but, with no customers around, the hexagonal seats and the glittering gold chandeliers lent the place an even more special feel. The crew of ten bustled about setting up the stage, and for the first time in a long time Carla felt a buzz.

The six costumes comprising three designer gowns and three cocktail dresses chosen for the shoot were sublimely beautiful, and when she took her place on the marker for the photographer, she couldn't stop the smile that curved her lips.

Javier came up behind her as she stood on the railing of the balcony that fed two wide, sweeping staircases. 'You seem pleased, *querida*.'

Her smile stretched, just as her heart had begun to expand with joy each time he used that endearment. 'I didn't think I'd enjoy this, but now that it's happening, I like it.'

'Why did you think you wouldn't enjoy it? You've done other sponsored shoots before.'

She shrugged, her gaze taking in the tiny platinum lights that glittered the dance floor. 'Yes, but wearing a watch or the latest ski jacket is different than this. This is a whole new experience.' An experience heightened by the man who stood so close, she could feel his warmth all around her; smell his powerfully unique scent. Both made her want to turn around, burrow into him and drown in that sensation.

She kept her ground, barely, as his arms rested on the railing on either side of her hips. 'In that case, enjoy it to the max. But don't lose sight of the depth of your talent. I've seen you skate. You may not have chosen that career for yourself, but you excel at it because it comes from your soul. Take a break if you need to—we'll work something out—but never forget the gift you've been given.'

Long after he'd walked away and the photos had been taken, his words lingered. And later that night, when the cadence of his lovemaking changed, his hitherto masterful possession gentling into a much more poignant claiming, she was left shaken, unable to separate reality from what her heart suddenly seemed to be yearning for—a sign that Javier saw this cluster of situations that had brought them together in a more meaningful light. But how could he?

He'd shaped his project after her—literally—but he was a man who collected trophies, who had homes around the world and more expensive toys than any one man could ever enjoy in a lifetime.

And you're just one bauble for him to possess briefly until he grows bored...

The harsh bruising to her heart was so immediate and terrifying, she gasped.

Javier's head jerked up from where he'd been trailing

post-coital kisses on her shoulder. 'What's wrong?' he de-manded.

Sucking in a breath, she shook her head quickly and raised herself up onto her elbows. 'Nothing.' She kissed him, seeking shameful refuge in the melting that filmed the pain. 'Nothing at all.'

CHAPTER TWELVE

NOTHING AT ALL.

She continued to recite those three words to herself throughout the frenzy of party preparations over the next three days. Relieved to see that Javier didn't mind her getting involved, she pulled on hostessing skills learned from an early age after her mother's departure. Back when her father had wanted to rub shoulders with the well-to-do without incurring the expense of it. Then later it'd been another way to tie her to his side, to control her, while basking in the limelight of her success.

He'd called them a *team*, and she'd convinced herself that meant *something*. Until it'd been far too late.

She strode out of the dressing room, where she'd been putting finishing touches to her make-up before the party, to the bedside table. Before she picked up her phone she knew there would be no message from her father.

The promise of funds had been well-received. Not so much the hold Javier had initially placed on the transmission of the money—with her approval—until her father had delivered on his promise to tell her about her mother. Her father's grim silence was meant to prolong her anguish. In the end, Carla had requested that Javier just release the money to him, but her father still hadn't called.

And the tension was succeeding in getting to her—

'Is there a reason you're staring at your phone when I need you downstairs with me?' came a semi-brusque query.

Setting her phone down, she turned. One of the things she'd quickly learned to accept was that Javier wanting what he wanted *when* he wanted wasn't something she could change any time soon. Another thing she couldn't change was her heart's crazy leap whenever her eyes connected with his. The ferocious intensity of his gaze seemed to have acquired an even pithier depth lately, as if he saw beneath her skin, to every unsettling emotion she didn't want him to glean. Carla wanted to believe she was succeeding in hiding her feelings, but a steady voice inside mocked her feeble attempts.

He reached her and captured her hands. 'Our guests are arriving.'

The collective statement caused yet another shifting of her emotional foundation. Watching him, she silently despaired at how effectively his every word and look battered at her defences; how her heart seemed to live for just such a moment, when he looked at her as if she really mattered to him.

'I'm ready,' she finally managed when she could speak past the trepidation clogging her throat.

His answer was to lift her hands away from her body, his appreciative scrutiny flooding her with idiotic pleasure. '*Sì*, you are. The gown is perfect on you,' he stated with pure, male satisfaction.

'*Grazie,*' she murmured.

The sleeveless red gown fitted her like a dream, a sleek confection of criss-crossed chiffon and silk that hugged her torso and hips and fell to her ankles in a gentle flare. She'd fallen in love with it the moment Javier had presented her with it this afternoon, despite the unease that had lanced through her at the thought that his claiming of her was attaining *absolute* proportions. His drawled observation that she hadn't packed for the party and didn't have time to go shopping had been meant to appease, except she'd glimpsed the barely concealed look of triumph on his face as he'd walked away after her acceptance of the gown. But even that hadn't been enough to dim her enjoyment of the garment.

The thought that she was escaping an oppressive prison for a gilded one made her heart lurch, until she reminded herself of the transient nature of her current situation. Pin-ning a smile on her face, she met his narrowing eyes. 'Shall we go?'

'Not just yet.'

Her eyes widened as he reached into his dinner jacket and pulled out a large, flat box. Before he opened it, she stepped back.

'Javier, no.'

A trace of displeasure gleamed in his eyes. 'It's my birthday, *mi amante*, you're not supposed to refuse me.' He opened the box to reveal a heart-meltingly gorgeous platinum chain from which a large teardrop diamond hung.

'And you're supposed to receive presents, not give them!' For reasons she couldn't fathom, the sight of the necklace seemed to compound her roiling emotions. 'This isn't necessary, Javier.'

'I don't do it out of necessity,' he drawled. 'Merely because it complements your dress. Feel free to return it at the end of the evening if you feel that strongly about it.' He plucked the chain from the velvet and waited expectantly.

With no choice but to argue, and keep their guests waiting, or give in gracefully, Carla turned around and lifted the newly styled fall of her hair. He secured the necklace, the cool stone resting between her breasts, then he stepped back. 'Oh, one thing I neglected to mention.'

She turned. 'Yes?'

He shrugged. 'Sadly, now that you've worn it, it's nonreturnable. It's not the vendor's policy, of course, but my own. So you're stuck with it.'

Speechless, she stared at him, watched a dark, wicked smile break over his face. It heated her blood and singed her insides as he tucked her arms into his and led her from the room. She was searching for an adequate comeback when they reached the double doors of the great room.

A different sort of trepidation hit her as she heard familiar voices. But that all changed when an additional voice sent her rushing in.

'Maria!'

The whine of the electrical wheelchair sounded over the soft background music as her friend turned at the sound of her name.

'There you are. We were thinking of sending out a search party for you.' Dark of complexion and as strikingly beautiful as her brother was handsome, Maria Angelis scrutinised Carla's face with wide and shrewd eyes as she rolled forward.

'You're a little early. Not that I mind at all.' Carla leaned down and hugged her friend, striving not to show the heartache that lingered at the edges of her interactions with Maria.

Maria, once a talented figure skater, had suffered a crippling fall as a result of being pushed past her training capabilities by Tyson Blackwell. Unlike Carla, Maria hadn't escaped with a simple broken wrist and a concussion. She'd severely damaged her vertebrae, resulting in permanent disability. It was the reason Draco Angelis had fought so strenuously to have Tyson Blackwell brought to justice.

Her gaze lifted past her friend's shoulder to see Javier shaking hands with Draco. The gesture was a touch tense, but Draco's fiancée, Rebel Daniels, made a comment that had both men chuckling.

Breathing slightly easier, Carla concentrated on her friend. 'How are you?'

'Much better now that bastard is on the brink of a long jail term.' Maria's voice held satisfaction and the same iron-hard will that had seen her through intense rehabilitation and eventual acceptance of her situation. It was the same will that had bolstered Carla when she'd been met with resistance from her father and Tyson Blackwell. 'Thank you for agreeing to press charges,' her friend added.

Carla shook her head. 'No, thank you for standing by me when I needed you.'

Maria quirked an eyebrow in a move acutely reminiscent of her brother's. 'Not sure about the standing part, but you're welcome.'

Shocked laughter barked out of Carla, and she leaned down and pressed a kiss to her friend's cheek. Before she could straighten, Maria added, 'Besides, if I could walk I'd be fighting you for your Spanish hottie. And that just wouldn't be fair.'

Unable to stem the blush that rose in her face, she stammered, 'I'm not...he's not—'

She clamped her lips shut as the trio approached. Rebel Daniels smiled and enfolded her in a big hug, easing the constriction that had clamped Carla's heart on seeing her.

'Rebel, I owe you an apology,' she started.

A hand sporting a huge diamond waved her words away. 'Bygones. For everything.' She cast an eye at Draco, then Javier. 'I know the fuller story about your father and Blackwell now, and I'm only sorry we didn't nail the bastard before he did that to you.' She nodded at Carla's wrist. 'But if you insist, I know how you can make it up to me.'

'Oh?'

She exchanged a bliss-filled look with Draco. 'Come to our wedding. Draco tells me you're out of commission for another few weeks. The wedding is next month. I'd love to have both you and Javier there. I kinda insist, actually.' She grinned unashamedly.

Carla's lips parted; she had every intention of making an appropriate refusal. By then she had no idea where she'd be. She would either still be with Javier, or, more likely, freshly released from her sojourn in his bed. In neither scenario could she envisage herself in a position to attend a wedding—

'We'd love to be there,' Javier replied in easy, confident tones.

Carla barely stopped her mouth from dropping open.

Rebel's breathtaking smile widened. 'Great! Now, Javier, I hear you're seriously into your tequila. Any chance of a slammer before the hordes descend on us?'

The gaze he'd levelled on Carla after his shocking re-

sponse to the wedding invitation lingered for another in-
finitesimal second before he nodded at Rebel. 'Of course.'

'Cut her off after one, Santino. I need her sober for the
meeting in the morning with the wedding co-ordinator *she*
insisted on hiring,' Draco drawled with only a hint of exasperation.

Rebel made a face. 'Just because you're a drill sergeant
doesn't mean you get to opt out of your own wedding planning. You'll sample the same amount of cake as I do, and
weigh in on the china patterns.'

'Go drink your slammer now, Arabella, before I embar-
rass us both by showing everyone here who's boss.'

Rebel laughed, but her cheeks flared with adorable colour
as she hooked her arm though Javier's. 'Come on, Maria,'
she invited her future sister-in-law.

Carla sensed Draco's presence beside her as they watched
Javier lead the ladies to the far side of the room where the
bar had been set up.

'Are you not interested in the tequila party?' she asked
the tall, dark man.

'No. I've already had a preview of Javier's tequila. It's the
best of the best, as usual. I've also seen the new bottle.' His
gaze reluctantly left his fiancée's laughing figure to connect
with Carla's. 'It's an…interesting change from the original
design. Anything I should know about?'

She shook her head, and saw Draco's gaze swing to her
new loose, layered hairstyle. His raised eyebrow caused her
colour to heighten. 'I'm fine, Draco.'

He watched her for several seconds, then nodded. 'Santino tells me the situation with your father isn't resolved yet.'

Carla felt a touch of irritation. 'You've been discussing
me?'

'His interest seems genuine, and I'm not about to argue
with that. So, your father?'

Pain lanced her heart. 'It's not resolved yet, but I'm han-
dling it.'

'Good.'

She managed a wobbly smile before voices filled the hall-way.

Catering to the never-ending stream of guests meant Carla didn't have time to dwell on Javier or whatever his interests were where she was concerned.

She caught a brief reprieve when the DJ cranked up the music and the guests flooded to the dance floor. She skimmed the room and caught sight of Javier engaged in conversation with two guests. About to glance away, she froze when his head snapped suddenly up and his gaze captured hers. Carla wasn't sure how long she stayed in place, a prisoner to his imposing regard.

She jumped as a hand clamped on her arm. 'Jeez, you two need to get a room. Or a whole resort. Whatever. Do me a favour and make eyes at each other later, okay?' Rebel laughed. 'I need to use the ladies' room and I don't trust anyone else with my fiancé. Dance with him until I get back?'

'Um…'

'Thanks! And tune him out if he starts with the overprotective big brother thing.' She grinned at Draco's narrow-eyed stare, then disappeared in the direction of the powder room.

Carla stepped into his arms, her cast-bound hand on his shoulder as he led her around the floor. 'I promise not to tune you out again,' she stated.

'You probably won't need me for anything other than business matters from now on.' He looked down at her, his imposing frame commanding her attention. 'You've come a long way, you and Maria, and I'm proud of you. But I'm still a phone call away if you need me.' His gaze swung over her head, to the side of the room where she could feel another set of intense eyes boring into her back as she danced with Draco. 'For anything. Understand?'

Tears prickled her eyes and clogged her throat. She managed a murmured '*grazie*' before a firm hand seized her waist.

'Mind if I cut in?' came a hard voice.

Another speculative expression crossed Draco's face. 'Not at all,' he drawled before he relinquished her and struck off in search of his fiancée.

'Once again I find you dancing with a man who is *not* me,' Javier stated through gritted teeth. Dark eyes scoured her face, then his mouth flattened in a harsh line before she was jerked against him. 'And you're on the verge of tears.' His snarl held a touch of bewilderment. 'Know this now, *querida*, my *progressive* attitude has its limits.'

Carla sighed, the need to throw her hands up in surrender weighing her down. With each moment that she'd acted as his hostess, each moment his gaze had met hers across the room tonight, she'd known she was fighting a battle she was doomed to lose. Whatever feelings she was developing for Javier, they wouldn't be easily discarded once he was done with her. Which meant that even as she gloried at being in his arms right now her foundations were fracturing, the tsunami of pain gathering strength somewhere beyond her sight and reach.

'If I didn't know better, I'd think you invited him here to test me.'

His nostrils flared. 'I didn't. But those tears aren't very reassuring, and I find myself in dire need of reassurance.'

Her breath hitched. Swaying close until their torsos met, she spiked her fingers through the silky hair at his nape and gripped tight enough to get his attention. Dark eyes clashed with hers and, throwing caution to the wind, she let her naked emotion show. 'What do I need to do to prove that I want you? Only you?'

His pupils dilated, his chest rising in a shuddering breath. 'I'm sure you can think of something.'

In the end there was only one way to prove herself, one language they both understood. In the early hours of the morning, when every last guest had been wined and dined and sent on their way, she kissed her way down Javier's lean, powerful body and revelled in the shudders that shook his frame.

Mounting him, she took him deep inside her, watched him fight his control for an age before he finally roared his release. Catching her to him, he murmured thick, incoherent words in Spanish. And she…barely stopped herself from saying words that had no place in what was happening between them. Clasping her arms around him, she held him tight till he drifted off to sleep.

Only then did she reach for her phone to read the message she'd returned upstairs to find waiting for her.

Funds received. If you want to know what happened to your mother come home. But come alone.

Javier told himself it was tiredness casting the shadows in Carla's eyes. He even managed to believe it for the better part of a week. She smiled when he walked into the room, engaged him fully and attentively in conversation, and lost herself completely in his arms each time desire whipped sharp and urgent between them.

But something was wrong. Her laughter wasn't quite as carefree and a fleeting expression of panic crossed her face when she thought he wasn't looking. Most telling of all, she'd begun to catch her hair up in that blasted knot again. Javier was certain she wasn't aware she was doing it. Each time he'd reached out to free it, she'd looked surprised. And a touch alarmed.

He gritted his teeth and tossed his pen onto his desk. Swivelling in his chair, he stared out at the New York skyline, wondering if geography was playing a part in the general sour mood he found himself in today.

After her last X-ray her doctor had agreed to remove her cast and replace it with a tensor bandage. She'd also conditionally freed Carla to work, and she'd wholeheartedly thrown herself into the tequila shoot. The test shots strewn across his desk were already perfect. He turned back and stared at the photos.

Dios, she was breathtaking. The pale gold skater leotard and gold-hued tights gave the illusion of her being nude, with the exception of the gold ice skates adoring her feet. Stunning green eyes, made up to deliver a sultry look, stared straight into the camera…into him…her legs parted wide enough to frame the life-size bottle as her fingers gripped its neck.

The results surpassed his every expectation. She was sexy, provocative enough to guarantee a mega-successful launch. The creative director had proclaimed herself happy with her so far and had progressed to the ice-skate shoot. In another forty-eight hours, the shoot would be over.

She would be back in New York with him. With her eyes still shadowed with emotions she was determined to hide from him.

Snarling a curse, he reached for the phone.

She answered on the second ring, with the same breathy excitement she'd met him with when he'd flown back to Miami at the end of each working day. Each time he'd hoped the shadows would be gone. Each time he'd looked deeper and found they'd grown.

'*Ciao*, Javier.'

'I have your test photos on my desk,' he said as a starter, because he didn't want to be met with a patently false *nothing* when he asked what was wrong.

'And?' she asked, a thin thread of dread lacing her voice.

'They're good.'

Her laughter held a tinge of relief. 'Just good? Jemma must have been exaggerating then when she said you loved them?'

He relaxed in his seat, a knot of tension unravelling from

his shoulders. 'Fine. They're great. How did the practice shoot go?'

'I'll let you be the judge of it. I detest watching myself on video. And there wasn't much actual skating involved. Just a lot of simulated moves and posing.'

Javier refrained from mentioning he had a copy of it awaiting his review on his laptop. He wasn't exactly sure why he hadn't been able to bring himself to watch it yet. 'You'll get my verdict soon enough,' he prevaricated.

'Are you on your way home?'

He heard the careful anticipation laced with the tiny trepidation and his fingers tightened around the phone. The urge to batter her defences, demand to know what she was hiding, powered through him. But he couldn't fight this battle. Not just yet.

'No. Not tonight.'

'What…umm…why?'

'My father got in touch. I guess the waiting game is over. I'm flying to Spain tonight.'

Silence punctuated by her soft breathing flowed over him. Javier wanted to demand her every thought, her every need. But he kept silent.

'How long will you be away?' she finally asked.

'Two days, three at the most. He has no bargaining chips remaining.' And he intended to drive that message home should his father decide to indulge in another useless ego trip.

'I hope you're successful,' she murmured.

All of a sudden, he'd had enough. Enough of dancing around their issues. Enough of the distance yawning between them. 'Come with me,' he suggested.

She gave a soft gasp that reached into him and settled around his heart. 'I can't. I would be sabotaging your project if I left now.'

'I don't care.'

'I do, and so should you.'

'Are you berating me?' he growled.

'I wouldn't dream of it,' she flung back.

'Are you at the ice rink?'

'*Sì*...yes.' The trepidation in her voice grew. 'I'm laced up and ready to go.'

'*Querida?*'

Her voice caught. 'Yes?'

'You're perfect. You'll be fine.'

A tiny broken sound escaped her. '*Grazie*. I... I needed that.' Voices murmured in the background. 'I have to go, Javier.'

The knot returned to his shoulder. Larger. Tighter. A similar one settled on his chest. 'I'll call you tonight.' He paused. 'Tell me you'll miss me,' he ordered softly.

A tiny sigh echoed in his ear, followed by taut silence. '*Sì*, I will miss you.'

The click of the line came far too soon. He wanted to call her back immediately. Wanted to hear her voice again.

Javier realised in the moment before he jumped to his feet and scooped up his laptop that he wanted a whole raft of things when it came to Carla Nardozzi. Things he had no right to demand but was going to anyway. As soon as he put his mother's ethereal and corporeal remains to rest.

Halfway across the Atlantic, he finally clicked on the link.

Her short, gold-spangled dress hugged her hips then flared out mid-thigh. Her hair flowed freely, just the way he liked it. Among the extras hired for the shoot, she shone bright and vibrant. She swayed to salsa music, arms outstretched to embrace life or a lover lucky enough to be allowed into her orbit.

Then, staring straight into the camera, she spoke the words. 'La Pasión. Taste the Edge. Live the Edge.'

He shut down the video, and the laptop, and swallowed hard as every ragged, unravelled sensation he'd felt around her finally made intense, mind-bending sense.

For three long years, she'd ruled his thoughts, peppered his every fleeting relationship. Not just because she had struck to the heart of his masculine pride. *Sí*, there had been that. He couldn't deny it. But more than that, Carla had struck something deeper, more substantial. Only he'd failed to see it till now.

His hand jerked towards the phone. But he pulled back. What he needed to say to her couldn't be done over the phone. He had to be there, in front of her, staring into her eyes.

He exhaled. A few days. A week, tops. Then this insanity would end.

Ten days later, Javier landed on the lawn of his Miami home and sprinted towards the house. The self-imposed radio silence from the moment he'd arrived in Menor Compostela had been hell itself, but he'd needed it to deal with the chaos he'd suddenly found himself embroiled in.

Vaulting up the shallow steps where the garden ended and the terrace began, he threw open the double doors and startled an advancing Constanza.

'Where is she?' he demanded as he crossed the room. His calls en route to the airport in Spain hadn't been answered. Neither had the ones he'd made on his plane heading home.

'*Señor?*'

'Carla. Is she upstairs?' he threw over his shoulder as he trotted into the hallway. He slowed as his housekeeper shook her head.

'*Lo siento, señor*, but the *señorita*, she's gone.'

His foot froze on the bottom step. 'What do you mean, *gone*?' Ice rolled down his spine even as he said the words. Because hadn't a part of him known? Hadn't a part of him suspected this would happen?

Futile anger congealed in his stomach as Constanza's gaze turned to pity. 'She left four days ago, *señor*.'

His breath punched through his throat. 'She's been gone

for over half a week and—?' And what? He'd given no explanation to his staff as to her presence in his life. As far as his employees were concerned, she was just the woman who'd been working for him by day and warming his bed at night. They'd afforded her respect because she'd been with him, but beyond that Carla might as well have been a treasured painting hung on a wall and admired but nothing else.

He slashed his fingers through his hair, his feet pounding the hallway as he paced back and forth. Belatedly, he realised his housekeeper was trying to get his attention.

'Yes?'

She reached into her pocket, warily extracted the folded envelope and held it out. Puzzled, Javier glanced at it. 'What's that?'

'Señorita Carla, she left it for you.'

CHAPTER THIRTEEN

'I NOW PRONOUNCE you husband and wife.'

Why did I come?

Why did he?

Her letter had been clear. More than clear. And his silence in the weeks after had all but shouted his acceptance of her need for no contact. So why was Javier sitting behind her in the church pew, his eyes glued to her back? She knew she wasn't deluding herself about the potency of his stare. He'd arrived ten minutes after the ceremony had started. She knew because the murmurs his presence had drawn had made her look behind her.

One look.

One ferocious, intensely rigid stare back from him, and she'd hastily straightened.

He hadn't joined in the hymns. Or snapped a photo of the stunning bride and groom sharing their first kiss. He'd remained, statue-still behind her, his attention riveted one hundred per cent on her.

The foolish wish that she'd worn her hair down was quickly squashed beneath more desperate anguish. The realisation on the night of his birthday party that she loved him had come as no real surprise to her. Nor had the inevitable acceptance that her love was doomed to bring her nothing but pain. She'd lost her head over him in record time. Or had that love been lying dormant for three years, her heart already his to possess the moment he'd possessed her?

Carla had spent far too many hours debating the whys and wherefores. Each had brought her to the same conclusion. There had never been one single hope of a future with Javier. Her tie to him should've begun and ended on paper.

Except it hadn't…

It had begun with her body and ended up in her soul—

'Are you going to sit there all day, pretending I don't exist?' his hard voice snarled in her ear.

Carla started. A quick glance showed the last of the wedding guests straggling out of the small island chapel where Draco and Rebel had married in his native Greece. Outside the sun blazed in its oblivious glory. Inside, she shivered, her heart leaping into her throat as she finally allowed herself to look at Javier.

His neatly trimmed five o'clock shadow accentuated his hollower cheekbones, his bespoke suit draped upon his lean body with an inherent grace and elegance reserved for demigods.

Standing, she faced him properly. 'Javier—'

'No. We're not doing this here. Two people have been lucky enough to find what they want in each other. I won't ruin their day.'

'Then why did you come?'

Dark brows clouded. *'Perdón?'*

'Despite my asking, no, *pleading*, with you to give me space, here you are. You could've stayed on the opposite side of the chapel. There are over five hundred guests here. We needn't have seen each other. And yet here you are.'

His nostrils flared, as if he couldn't believe the words spilling from her lips. 'Because you owe me an explanation. And because you chose to vanish off the face of the earth for the past three weeks. *That is why!'*

Her heart slammed into her stomach. 'My letter wasn't enough?'

His hand slashed the air. 'Your letter was—' He stopped, then shook his head. 'I won't be drawn into this here with you, Carla. We will go outside and wish the happy couple well. We will stay for a glass or two of champagne. I might even bring myself to dance with you. But you and I will leave this island together. Tonight. And we will settle this once and for all.'

He whirled from her, his designer shoes clicking in perfect staccato as he headed outside.

Following him, Carla saw heads turn as he joined the wedding party. Handshakes and kisses were exchanged with the bride and groom. Then he was turning towards her once more. Icy eyes locked on hers as he held out his hand to her. But within the depths, Carla caught an edgy vulnerability, a faint light that attempted to jump-start her hopes. Carla berated herself for reading signs where there were none.

His jaw turned to granite at her hesitation.

'For heaven's sake, Carla. If you don't grab onto that and hold on with everything you've got, I damn well will.'

The exasperated whisper came from beside her. She looked down to see Maria glaring at her. 'Go, dammit.'

She went. Not because she truly believed there was something to grab onto. But because before her heart shrivelled up and deserted her for the final time, she wanted to touch Javier. Selfishly feel his vibrant skin against hers one last time.

His fingers closed over hers and her blood kicked back into her veins.

This is an illusion. This is temporary.

Everything about this is temporary.

But she took her seat next to him at the great wedding feast. Clinked glasses with him for the wedding toast. Smashed plates and applauded Draco and Rebel's first dance.

Javier didn't offer to dance with her after all. Which was just as well. Her heart had dropped to her toes by the time Rebel left to change for her honeymoon trip.

'Excuse me,' she murmured, then fled before Javier could stop her.

She found Draco momentarily alone in one corner of the many terraces that graced his multi-storeyed island villa.

'Draco.'

He turned, his smile blisteringly radiant, before he frowned. Catching her by the arm, he drew his thumb down her cheek. 'Carla, are you all right?'

She blinked back tears that had been clogged in her throat for hours. 'Please, don't worry about me. Today belongs to you. I'll find my own way to be okay. I promise.'

His frown deepened. 'Carla...'

She stood on tiptoe and hastily placed a kiss on his cheek. 'Give my love to Rebel.'

Turning, she found Javier standing six feet away. The bleakness that lanced his features tore at her. Again hope threatened to rise.

But she was tired. And battered.

She walked past him, through the ballroom overlooking sheer cliffs and a glorious sunset. She heard him behind her but didn't stop until she reached the lift. He entered after her, staying on one side of the small car, his arms folded as he stared straight ahead.

It was only as she stood beneath the pillared courtyard awaiting the buggy that would take her to the chopper reserved to fly guests back to the mainland that he spoke.

'Where have you been these past few weeks, Carla?'

She contemplated silence. Talking was dangerous. It fed an urge to reveal innermost desires that had no chance of birth, never mind growth. But this was a safe subject that had nothing to do with her breaking heart. 'My mother bought a cottage near Maidstone, on the English coast where she grew up. She left it to me. I put it on the market when my father...when I thought I'd need the funds. Three weeks ago the agents contacted me with an offer. I came down with the intention to clear it out.'

'But you decided a cottage in the middle of nowhere was the perfect hiding spot?'

'I wasn't hiding.'

The buggy arrived. He helped her into it, then took his place next to her. From shoulder to thigh, their bodies connected. Carla lost the power of speech. And Javier didn't seem inclined to continue their conversation as they were driven towards the aircraft area.

When the buggy started to slow down beside the chopper, Javier tapped the valet on the shoulder. 'Take us to the airstrip.'

'But I'm going to the mainland to catch my flight back to England.'

His mouth flattened. 'You can catch a flight with me. Or we can talk on my plane before you catch your flight. Either way, we're talking.'

'Javier, this is pointless.'

A look of actual pain crossed his face, making her want to take back her words. But short of the definitive words or the commitment from him whose twin was lodged in her heart, she knew nothing would ease her heartache. And being with him, like this, was turning out to be far worse than she'd imagined.

The buggy arrived at the steps of his plane. He got out and waited, his eyes hard and unmoving on hers.

To prolong this would be to prolong her pain. She alighted and climbed the steps into the plane.

Save a single attendant, there was no sign of Javier's crew. Which was good because she didn't want witnesses to her heartache.

The plane took off in record time. The moment the seatbelt sign flashed off, Javier surged to his feet.

He paced the space in front of her for terse minutes, before he leaned over her chair.

'What must I do to prove to you that I can be worthy of you? How can I even do that if you won't give me a chance?'

Carla's mouth dropped open. 'What are you talking about?'

Reaching into his jacket, he produced a familiar-looking sheet. 'I'm talking about this,' he snarled. 'Your *Dear John* letter.'

'You…kept it?'

Incredulity lightened his eyes. 'That's what interests you in all this? Whether or not I kept your letter?'

He slammed the sheet on the table next to her. 'Explain it, *por favor.*'

She licked lips gone dry with trepidation. 'Which part?'

'All of it!'

Carla stared down at the words that had killed her to write, her limbs leaden as she reached for the single, most difficult thing she'd ever had to do.

Javier,

I returned to the ice today, and you were right. I love it. It's in my blood. But I'm not in love with it. Not at the moment. Maybe it will return. Maybe it won't. I need to give it time.

There's an old saying about loving something and letting it go, right? But I allowed myself to love it again for the sake of your shoot. I hope you like the result. If you don't... I'm sorry, but I'm done. Done faking. Done pretending I don't want what I want.

I deserve better than that. We both do. I still intend to fulfil my endorsement obligations to you. But I think it would be best if I deal with your team going forward. You will most likely be angry with me, but I hope you grant me this clean break.

For all that has gone before, I'm sorry. But please, let me be.

Carla

The paper disappeared as he snatched it back up. A peculiar fire blazed in his eyes. 'You're done *faking*? Exactly which part did you fake with me? The days when you couldn't stop smiling at each new experience we shared, or the nights you came apart in my arms?' he finished, his voice a hoarse, bleak rasp.

Her breath shook out in searing recollection. She reached out, for what, she didn't know, but he turned in a tight, horribly graceless pace.

'You want what you want? How am I supposed to have a chance of offering myself up to help you achieve it when you disappear without trace?'

'I didn't think you'd want me to stay, knowing...'

He stopped. 'Knowing what?'

She shook her head. 'It doesn't matter. You said you'd be gone for a few days...that you'd call. You didn't...'

'So you took it as an excuse to bail? When will you stop running from me? From *us*?' He stared down at her, a stiff entreaty in his eyes, before he shook his head. 'Maybe I'm truly insane. I have to be, don't I, to keep throwing myself at your feet when you don't want me?'

She gasped. 'Javier—'

'You're right. You deserve better. I just haven't been self-less enough to see it.' He balled the letter and thrust it into his pocket, before he gripped his own nape in a merciless hold. 'I didn't call you because my father was in the middle of having a stroke when I arrived.'

'What?'

'He survived, but he's lost the power of speech and will most likely be wheelchair-bound for the rest of his life.'

'I... I don't know what to say.'

His mouth twisted. 'I think you've said plenty. Anyway, under his power of attorney, his eldest son has assumed his responsibilities. I was able to negotiate with him. He signed the document allowing my mother to be buried with her family.'

She stood and moved towards him. 'I'm so pleased this is over for you. That you both have closure.'

He inclined his head, but the mask of weariness and pain didn't dissipate. When his gaze lifted, his eyes held pools of deep anguish. 'What did I do that was so unforgivable, Carla? Was it forcing you to be my mistress? You didn't sleep with me against your will, I *know* that.'

She reached out and touched him, unable to abide his

pain. 'No, it wasn't that. It was never that. I left because I had to. I stayed gone because—'

'What do you mean you *had to*?'

'My father texted me on the night of your party. He was ready to tell me what happened to my mother.'

'Why didn't you tell me? I would've taken you—'

'That's just what he didn't want. He wanted me to come alone. I was terrified it meant the worst. That he'd killed her in a rage because I'd asked her to intervene with him on my behalf.'

'And did it?'

She shook her head, the relief of finally being able to put it behind her easing her heartache. 'It was an accident. Caused because they were rowing, and she was trying to get away from him, but it was an accident. She stormed out of the house and didn't watch were she was going. She slipped and hit her head going into the pool. My father had security cameras installed when he started buying expensive art. I… couldn't bring myself to watch all of it, but I saw enough to know he was telling the truth…'

'And he kept all this from you because…?'

She shrugged, although the pain of that knowledge deadened her limbs. As did the pain of her decision to walk away from her father, once and for all. Somewhere down the line, she might learn to forgive him for some of the things he'd done, but right now she was too raw to even bear the thought of him. 'It was just another way for him to control me, and he took it.'

Javier cursed, long and dark. His hand jerked out, as if to reach for her. At the last moment, it dropped to his side. 'You said you left because you had to go. What kept you from coming back?' he asked in a dead voice.

'You.'

'*Sí*, of course. The problem has always been me.'

'Yes, it has. Loving you has been a big problem for me. But living without you will be an even greater one.'

He paled. All colour left his vibrant face as he stood thirty thousand feet up in the air. 'You...' He shook his head. '*No entiendo*. I don't understand.'

She closed the distance between them and cradled his face in her hands. 'I didn't come back to you because I thought you only wanted me for the short term. I couldn't stand the thought of staying and loving you only to be cast aside sooner or later.'

Feverish eyes examined her for an age, before he shut his eyes in disbelief. 'I've loved you for three desperate years, *querida*. You ripped my heart out when you walked away from me that morning. After that I tried every means possible to get you back in my life. And now you...you...' He groaned and slanted his mouth over hers. The kiss wasn't gentle or sweet. It was three years of ravaging want and passionate need plugged full bore into their beings.

When he raised his head, they both gasped for air. Without giving her a chance to recover, he swung her into his arms and headed for the master suite at the back of the plane.

Clothes ripped in a frenzy of impatient desire. Fingers locked in her hair and pulled out pins. 'You're not allowed to wear your hair up again. Ever.' He caught her by the waist and rushed her to the bed.

Laughter, pure and joyous, ripped from her throat. 'What about when I'm competing?'

'You've decided to go back to the ice?'

'Not just yet. I want to enjoy being with you for a little bit. But I feel my love for it returning every day.'

He stretched out beside her and caught her face in his hand. 'It will be more glorious than ever, *mi amor*. And before that we will make up for every single day we've wasted thus far.'

Her back arched off the bed as he trailed his hand down her body. 'And how do you propose to do that?' she rasped in a voice heavy with desire.

'By signing you to another contract, of course.' He surged above her and parted her thighs.

'What type of contract?'

'A lifelong one, where you wear my ring and take my name. And where I get to worship you every night and love you every day,' he responded, his voice guttural with need. 'Do you accept?'

Tears filled her eyes. 'I accept. You were my first and my only, and I vow to be yours for ever.'

With pure adulation lighting his eyes, he entered her with one smooth thrust.

'*Lo ti adoro*, Javier.'

'As do I, *mi amor*. Never, ever doubt it.'

* * * * *

Don't miss Maya Blake's next story,
Book 2 of THE BILLIONAIRE'S LEGACY *series*
THE DI SIONE SECRET BABY
Available August 2016

In the meantime, don't miss
Lynne Graham's 100th book!
BOUGHT FOR THE GREEK'S REVENGE
Also available this month

MILLS & BOON®
Hardback – June 2016

ROMANCE

Bought for the Greek's Revenge	Lynne Graham
An Heir to Make a Marriage	Abby Green
The Greek's Nine-Month Redemption	Maisey Yates
Expecting a Royal Scandal	Caitlin Crews
Return of the Untamed Billionaire	Carol Marinelli
Signed Over to Santino	Maya Blake
Wedded, Bedded, Betrayed	Michelle Smart
The Surprise Conti Child	Tara Pammi
The Greek's Nine-Month Surprise	Jennifer Faye
A Baby to Save Their Marriage	Scarlet Wilson
Stranded with Her Rescuer	Nikki Logan
Expecting the Fellani Heir	Lucy Gordon
The Prince and the Midwife	Robin Gianna
His Pregnant Sleeping Beauty	Lynne Marshall
One Night, Twin Consequences	Annie O'Neil
Twin Surprise for the Single Doc	Susanne Hampton
The Doctor's Forbidden Fling	Karin Baine
The Army Doc's Secret Wife	Charlotte Hawkes
A Pregnancy Scandal	Kat Cantrell
A Bride for the Boss	Maureen Child

MILLS & BOON®
Large Print – June 2016

ROMANCE

Leonetti's Housekeeper Bride	Lynne Graham
The Surprise De Angelis Baby	Cathy Williams
Castelli's Virgin Widow	Caitlin Crews
The Consequence He Must Claim	Dani Collins
Helios Crowns His Mistress	Michelle Smart
Illicit Night with the Greek	Susanna Carr
The Sheikh's Pregnant Prisoner	Tara Pammi
Saved by the CEO	Barbara Wallace
Pregnant with a Royal Baby!	Susan Meier
A Deal to Mend Their Marriage	Michelle Douglas
Swept into the Rich Man's World	Katrina Cudmore

HISTORICAL

Marriage Made in Rebellion	Sophia James
A Too Convenient Marriage	Georgie Lee
Redemption of the Rake	Elizabeth Beacon
Saving Marina	Lauri Robinson
The Notorious Countess	Liz Tyner

MEDICAL

Playboy Doc's Mistletoe Kiss	Tina Beckett
Her Doctor's Christmas Proposal	Louisa George
From Christmas to Forever?	Marion Lennox
A Mummy to Make Christmas	Susanne Hampton
Miracle Under the Mistletoe	Jennifer Taylor
His Christmas Bride-to-Be	Abigail Gordon

0516 GEN STD LP